MISS CROSS

& OTHER STORIES

Norman Schwenk (1935-2023) was a writer and teacher from Lincoln, Nebraska in the United States. A love of reading and writing poems infused his childhood and intending to work as a teacher, he took a first degree at Nebraska Wesleyan University, and then enrolled as a postgraduate in American Studies at the University of Pennsylvania in Philadelphia, where he was made a teaching and research assistant in English. In 1963 he won a Fulbright Award from the U.S. State Department, and for the next five years he was a Fulbright Lecturer in English at Uppsala University in Sweden. He moved to Wales in 1965, having been appointed lecturer in American Literature at Cardiff University. He later became head of a thriving creative writing programme developing and influencing a diverse group of many talents.

Love and mortality were enduring themes for Schwenk including his fine collection *The Black Goddess* (1990) through to his selected poems in 2016. He also had a playful side to writing which included a series of chapbooks of comic verse exploring popular forms including *How To Pronounce Welsh Place Names*, a collection of limericks.

He retired from full-time teaching in 2002 which gave him more time to concentrate on his own work. In 2004 he co-edited with Anne Cluysenaar, an anthology of poems about St Melangell, *The Hare that Hides Within*. In 2005 he published *The More Deceived: Poems about Love and Lovers*; in 2010 *Cadillac Temple: Haiku Sequences*; and in 2015, *Book of Songs*, a collection of song lyrics. He wrote and published poetry throughout his adult life but only began writing prose in his 60s. He was working on *Miss Cross and Other Stories* over many years with his wife, the writer, Deborah Kay Davies as editor.

MISS CROSS

& OTHER STORIES

Norman Schwenk

PARTHIAN

Parthian, Cardigan SA43 1ED
www.parthianbooks.com
© Norman Schwenk 2023
Print ISBN: 9781914595714
Ebook ISBN: 978-1-914595-75-2
Editor: Deborah Kay Davies
Cover Design: Syncopated Pandemonium
Typeset by Elaine Sharples
Printed by 4edge Limited
Published with the financial support of the Books Council of Wales
British Library Cataloguing in Publication Data
A cataloguing record for this book is available from the British Library.
Printed on FSC accredited paper

For Deborah

CONTENTS

Acknowledgements   viii

life is crazy, but hang on in there -
Introduction by Deborah Kay Davies   ix

Miss Cross   1

Catman   12

Fred   18

Perry   23

Purse   32

Dancing Bear   35

Love Rat   38

Captain Flint   44

Down in the Bracken   53

Who's There?   61

Fay   73

Roach   77

Fairest Creatures   82

Patient   90

Piranhas   99

Velma   106

My Dog Can Talk   115

ACKNOWLEDGEMENTS

Thanks again to Norman's book designer and faithful friend, Richard Cox.

Thanks to dear Roger Ellis and Andrea Macintyre for their unstinting love and support.

Thanks also to Nigel Arrighi for his IT knowledge and patience with my cluelessness.

Thanks to the Edgeworks of old.

Thanks to Richard Davies at Parthian Books for the support he has shown Norman's work over the years, and especially now, in the publishing of this last book.

Thanks also to Gina Rathbone and Elaine Sharples.

LIFE IS CRAZY, BUT HANG ON IN THERE

My husband Norman Schwenk worked on these short stories for many years. He first began in the early 2000s, when we were part of a wonderful writing group called Edgeworks. Norm had been the instigator of this group in its first manifestation at Cardiff University in the 90s, where it was invaluable to the writers who taught there. He thought of himself as a poet, and for the most part that was what he did – wrote poems and haiku – but sometime during the 2000s he embarked on this collection. Over the years he would push these stories onto the back burner whilst he worked on his poetry, and then move them forward over the heat again. All through this long, seemingly leisurely process (he always made things look easy) I was with him. I looked at each new story, and commented, and sometimes he didn't like what I had to say, and sometimes he knew I was right and he would work some more. He stuck with these stories through the years, and so, of course, did I.

Over the last five years, as Norman became less able, he put them aside, but they were always on his mind. He wished for their launch to be in the year of his 88th birthday, and Richard Davies, Parthian, has made this possible. I know he would be so pleased.

They represent for me, among many things, the bracing, fascinating years we had, writing side by side. His unshaken belief in the supreme importance of getting on with our writing influenced me in so many positive ways. Now I am alone, editing his work. He isn't here to help me, but all he taught me, so unfussily and kindly, is foremost in my mind; I feel very lucky. And it has been wonderful to revisit them. They are weirder, and funnier and wiser than I even remember. He understood and was patient with the quirks and foibles of people – after all he was aware he shared them. That basic understanding of people with their nutty lives and hopeful floundering for love and meaning, permeate these strange, charming stories; the animals are the only sane ones.

Norm specially loved dogs and cats, and like most people, appreciated all animals great and small. Weaving their enigmatic way through these stories you will encounter lovelorn rats, spectral cats, peckish elephants, clever parrots and murderous horses. There is a mechanical bear and a dog who talks. These animals serve variously as familiars, emissaries, co-conspirators, or harbingers for both good and evil. They stand for many things, but what is true for all of them is the way, through their essential innocence, they change the often clueless, mostly flawed human characters Norman created. Through these tales I think he is saying wryly, hey, you guys, life is crazy, but hang on in there and do the best you can.

Deborah Kay Davies
Cardiff, 2023

MISS CROSS

'Vera, take the children to the story corner, please, and keep them away from the windows. Give me 10 minutes.' Miss Cross was whispering – unusual for her. She taught the children never to whisper, and she was the kind of head teacher who led by example.

Vera had enough experience not to dither or flap, just to do it. She caught the note of disciplined alarm in her young boss's voice, and knew she did not panic for nothing. Miss Cross took one more look out the window and headed for the door. She had to work quickly. In half an hour the children would be going home, and in ten or fifteen minutes mothers and fathers would be assembling to pick them up. She walked swiftly round the corner of the school, through the gate and onto the grass verge by the school-crossing. She stood for a moment and stared at the small, inchoate mound of grey fur mashed onto the tarmac. Someone's pet. Tears made her eyes itch, and a solid knot formed in her throat. She remembered her little mongrel, Pearl, who had been run over when she was ten. Miss Cross took a deep breath and tried to think.

Cars swished past in that unrelenting way traffic has. Some drivers slowed to glance at the small woman standing there, since she looked about to cross: a few men paused to gawp because she was a bit of all right, but none noticed the lump of matted hair that fixed her attention.

Miss Cross had just passed an exasperating half hour phoning round to council services – everything from Police to Fire, Cleansing to Animal Shelter – hoping to find someone who would come quickly and clear away poor Dusty or Pepsi, whatever the name was on the bent metal tag just visible in the fur. Cleansing had promised to come tomorrow. Too late. No one seemed to understand the distress that would overwhelm some of her little charges when they stepped onto the crossing and saw the tiny, mangled corpse. In the distance Miss Cross could see Brenda, the lollipop lady, on her way to mind the crossing. This focussed her thoughts. Brenda was certain to be unhelpful, and she had a knack for making you feel everything was your fault.

Miss Cross marched round to the back of the school, took out her heavy ring of keys and unlocked the cupboard where the tools were stored. The scoop shovel was long gone, stolen in one of the frequent raids on the school – the police regularly called her out in the depths of night – but there was still a venerable spade with a broken handle. Tooled up with spade and black plastic bin bag, she walked round to the front again and walked onto the crossing, stopping the honking traffic. Brenda had arrived by now, as a mute, baleful witness.

'It's good there's no blood,' thought Miss Cross. She ignored the gaping drivers who crawled past – one actually whistled as she bent over – and studied how best to approach the task. At first, squinting from the school window, she thought it might have been a cat, but close up she was now sure, from the texture of the tail, which was still intact, that it had recently been a dog. There was no address or phone number on the tag, and she could not read the name, which had been scratched on by hand.

Miss Cross positioned one foot on the bag so it would not blow away, then slid the spade along the tarmac until the small body was more or less balanced on the blade. She marvelled at the construction of bodies. How could one, squashed so flat and so completely floppy, somehow keep its shape? Even the little head was flattened. It dangled off the spade on the end of a broken neck. At this point the reasonable thing would have been to ask Brenda to hold the bag for her. She could just hear Brenda say, 'Nothing to do with me,' her favourite phrase. Now, holding the bag with her left hand, she negotiated the spade with her right and, with a single deft movement, as if she had been shovelling cadavers all her life, popped it in and out of sight. The grace of this manoeuvre surprised even Miss Cross. There was a greasy spot where the body had lain, which looked both slippery and sticky. She took a tissue out of her sleeve and wiped it round to little effect. Then she straightened up and tied the top of the bag, swallowing a small spurt of vomit which had risen to her mouth. Finally, disciplining herself not to glare at Brenda, she left the public arena of the crossing, walked briskly round the back, leaned against a wall and pondered what to do next.

A proper grave was out of the question. The nursery school ground had been covered almost entirely in plastic cushion, and the children were certain to spot anything unusual. It would have to go into one of the giant steel wheelie bins in front of her. She stepped up to one, raised the cover and looked in. A stale, unidentifiable stench wafted over her as she peered in trying to see the bottom. How on earth did the cleaners manage? The bins were efficiently designed for emptying into council lorries, but awkward to handle for human beings. The cover alone seemed to weigh a ton. Her sad parcel hit the bottom with a soft splash. Miss Cross exhaled profoundly, then took her anger out on the old spade, slinging it back in the cupboard and slamming the door like a sheriff jailing a bandit. As she walked round the front she remembered the dead dog story that was part of family legend. A favourite aunt of hers had woken one morning to discover her little old dog had died in the night. The aunt lived in a block of flats in London and couldn't bear to put the body out with rubbish. She decided to take it back to the family farm and bury it there. So she packed it in a suitcase and went straight to the railway station. A nice man at the station offered to help with her heavy suitcase, but while she was buying a ticket the nice man ran off. She was left to imagine the horrors of what might have happened to the body of her pet. Her only consolation was to imagine also the look on the thief's face when he opened her suitcase.

Inside the school you'd never have known there was an emergency. Blessed Vera was coping. The children were clearly enjoying their extended version of 'Gelert', the tragic tale of the heroically faithful dog. Miss Cross spotted little Rosie Todd, with her thick glasses and cross-eyes, her face shining. She wondered how Rosie, so proud and sensitive, would have dealt with seeing the body in the road.

But when Miss Cross glanced out the window again she spotted Brenda marching toward the school, holding her lollipop like a pikestaff at the ready. What could have induced Brenda to leave her post? Shuffling beside her was a crumpled woman with a puffy red face who carried a large box of tissues. Miss Cross nipped over to the entrance and managed to head them off.

'What is it, Brenda?' she said, standing with her back to the door.

'This is my friend, Pat,' announced Brenda. 'The police say you've got her dog.'

Miss Cross noticed their conversation was already attracting attention. A few mothers and fathers had gathered at the fence. She could imagine the questions at tomorrow's parents' evening.

'Brenda, I think you'd better go back to your crossing,' she said. 'Pat, I'm Rebecca. We can talk in my office.'

Brenda opened her mouth to speak, but Miss Cross gave her a look; Brenda did an about-face and retreated.

Miss Cross led Pat to her office, where she explained about the dog on the crossing as gently as she could. Her remarks were punctuated by ripping sounds and toots as Pat removed tissues from the box, mopped her tears and blew her nose. Pat's dog was Georgie, a small white poodle she was convinced had been stolen by dog thieves. She was maddeningly vague about his collar and tag. Miss Cross had to admit the dog on the crossing could once have been a white poodle. If she pressed Pat for more complete information, though, it seemed to make her cry even louder, so she promised to bring the body in where Pat could have a look. She didn't say it was dumped in a wheelie bin. As Miss Cross walked through the schoolroom on her way back to the bins, she noticed Vera was at the question-and-answer stage, winding up her story in preparation for the final song.

5

Little Mohammed Clark caught her eye, his upper lip as always shining with nasal slime; surely her efforts were worthwhile, saving him a nightmare or two – he was such a tender-hearted softie, who loved Miss Cross with utter devotion.

Back at the bins she struggled to remember which one she'd chucked the bag in. The smell was no help. They all had the same unrecognisably foul odour, one that didn't make you jump with revulsion but drove you back slowly. She stood on tiptoe – as a career woman she had to contend with the handicap of being petite as well as pretty – and peered in the middle bin. She saw lots of black bags, and there it was; she was quite certain, even though all the bags looked very much the same. She got a rickety stepladder out of the cupboard, together with a grizzled old floor brush, climbed up and threw back the huge lid, which sheared off its hinge and fell to the concrete with a crash. Miss Cross stopped and listened. She could hear the children singing 'She'll Be Coming Round the Mountain'. They always had a song at the end of the day – nice for the parents while they were waiting. She started fishing with the brush, trying to hoist the bag up where she could catch hold of it. This didn't work. The bags were slippery from a pool of rancid water at the bottom. She then laid the brush across the top of the bin so she could grip it like an acrobat, reaching down with her short arms and groping with her small hands. Just as she touched the chosen bag, she teetered on the stepladder, overbalanced and pitched in head first.

Anyone peering around the corner of the school at this moment, as indeed Brenda was, would have seen a slim set of ankles and a neat pair of beige court shoes waggling just above the rim of the bin. Miss Cross had landed on the layer of bags and was not injured, though she would nurse a painful shoulder for a few days, and a sore nose where the brush had struck her. She stood up inside the bin, wiped off her neat brown suit, readjusted the scarf round her throat and ascertained that her tights were well-laddered. She checked an impulse to tears, holding her breath and swallowing hard. Then she picked up the bag she'd been angling for and opened it. All-purpose trash. God help me if I'm in the wrong bin, she said almost out loud. (What she did say out loud was, 'balls'.) A quick rummage produced the right bag, though, and Miss Cross dropped it over the side along with her shoes and started struggling to climb out. She could feel hysteria rising in her and concentrated hard on practical things. She made a pedestal of bags, threw one shapely leg over the rim, then the other and slid down onto the concrete. As she did she noted Brenda spying on her round the corner. Brenda had traffic backed up for a hundred yards or more, because standing out on the crossing gave her the best view. Then, seeing that Miss Cross saw her, she resumed conscientious lollipop duty. Miss Cross had just got her shoes back on when a worried Vera appeared and asked, please, would she come and deal with some council workmen who said she'd phoned them. They were causing a ruction. Miss Cross, bag in hand, was confronted at the school door by two men wearing wheel-clamp-yellow council jackets that said CLEANSING. One was large and burly, the other small and scrawny.

'Where's the dead dog!' shouted the big one, so everyone could hear. Parents and children were milling around putting coats on.

'We were called here on emergency,' said the little one. 'Dead dog on the crossing.' Miss Cross didn't dare look at the children, but she could sense their agitation, like a kettle starting to boil. She opened her mouth to speak to the workmen and felt the bag snatched out of her hand. Behind her the pathetic Pat was untying the bag so as to display its contents to the massed gathering. Miss Cross tried to snatch the bag back and there was an unseemly grapple. 'Please! Let's open it in my office,' hissed Miss Cross. 'You're upsetting the children.'

Pat burst into sobs, still clutching the bag.

'Is that the dead dog?' shouted the burly workman.

Miss Cross turned on him. 'I've cleaned the crossing myself,' she said. 'You're too late. Now please go.'

'So who's going to sign our job sheet?' said the scrawny one. 'You've wasted our time.'

Miss Cross scrawled on the proffered job sheet and turned her back on the men, only to behold Pat, surrounded by children, opening the bag. As the dab of dead fluff came into view there was a chorus of wails, followed by tears and general chaos. Vera was doing her best to shepherd children out the door and match them up with the right parents.

'Miss Cross!' She could hear the grating voice of Ms Viner at her elbow, a parent who never missed a chance to complain. 'Miss Cross, I must protest. This is outrageous.'

Miss Cross turned to Ms Viner and looked her in the eye until Ms Viner looked away. She noticed Ms Viner had a bright yellow spot on the end of her nose, which seemed sufficient revenge for the day and helped Miss Cross resist an impulse to kick her in the shins.

'I'll explain at the parents' evening tomorrow night,' she said, her voice even and smooth. 'Now please excuse me.' Small as she was, Miss Cross gathered up Pat and the bag, hauled them into her office and shut the door on the noise. She started to give Pat a telling off but didn't have the heart and ended up comforting her.

'Sorry, Rebecca,' Pat kept saying. 'I've caused you such trouble. You've been so good.'

'It's your little dog, is it?' said Mrs Cross. 'Georgie?'

'No, it isn't,' Pat blubbered. 'Nothing like him.'

A small explosion of rage detonated inside Miss Cross, but there was not a flicker of an outward sign. Just then Rosie Todd's father barged into the office without knocking, clearly upset. Oh, no, thought Miss Cross, I'm losing even the supportive ones. His voice trembled as he spoke.

'Miss Cross, can you please explain why my child was handed over to me in tears? What is going on in this school of yours?'

'I do apologise, Mr Todd. I can't discuss it now. I'll make an announcement at parents' evening.'

Mr Todd hesitated. 'I'm afraid that's all I can say for now.' She indicated the weeping Pat, glad to be able to use her as an excuse.

'Very well,' said Mr Todd, who left in confusion.

Pat started sobbing even louder, going on about what trouble she'd caused and how kind Miss Cross was. Stonily, Miss Cross left her to it and went to help Vera clear up. Before long Brenda arrived to collect her friend, and they limped away, Brenda helping Pat down the path as if she'd broken a leg.

Before Vera went home Miss Cross apologised for not keeping her better informed about the dog. Vera shrugged and laughed – not a nervous laugh, but a loud, genuine, Vera laugh.

'I loved it when you sent those council blokes packing,' said Vera. 'We'll talk to the kids about it tomorrow. They'll understand.'

'Yes,' said Miss Cross. 'And the parents.' Her heart sank at the thought.

'I know you well enough to do some grooming, don't I?' said Vera unexpectedly, and reached over and touched Miss Cross's shoulder. Then Vera held out her hand and laughed again. In her palm was what looked like a large sprig of parsley.

'A bit of garnish from round the back, I expect,' said Vera.

After Vera had gone Miss Cross stood alone looking out the window, all her nerves singing, waiting for calm to return. Maybe they ought to have a burial tomorrow. Would it be wise? Some of the parents would protest, perhaps quite rightly. But now that they had all seen the dead dog? She couldn't say it had gone out with the garbage. Just then, over the crossing and up the path to the school, shambled a pleasant-looking young man in scruffy clothes. His body was deformed in some way, but Miss Cross couldn't quite make out how. She went to the door to meet him.

'Sorry to trouble you,' he said, in a warm, dry voice. 'The police say you might have the remains of my dog, Bandy. He got out this morning. My fault. He hasn't a clue about cars.'

Miss Cross sighed and smiled. 'The police seem to think I run a canine morgue,' she said. 'You're welcome to have a look. I'm afraid the body's in a rubbish bag.'

'He's white, with a black band round the base of his tail,' said the man. 'Like a napkin ring.'

She went into her office and got the bag out of the desk drawer where she'd stowed it while placating Pat. The man looked inside. Miss Cross noticed he used only one hand.

'That's Bandy,' he said, swallowing. 'Poor little sod.'

'I'm sorry,' said Miss Cross. 'I'm so sorry.'

'Thanks,' said the man. They stood facing each other, the young man choked with feeling. Miss Cross could now see he had only one arm. He knelt beside the bag.

'Is he going to pray?' she thought. 'Should I kneel too?'

With his one arm the man reached inside the sleeve of the other. There was a small whirring sound, and a prosthetic arm slowly reeled out of the sleeve and grasped the top of the bag. The arm was a complicated structure which looked like it might have been made from antique toys. The man looked up and smiled. 'Like it?' he said. 'I made it myself.'

Miss Cross gaped at him, speechless, and smiled weakly. He hooked the bag onto the mechanical arm, shook her hand with the other and went out. Miss Cross started to snicker hysterically, but controlled herself. Then quietly she began to cry.

CATMAN

Cat Man wasn't a remarkable-looking old guy. You wouldn't have picked him out of a crowd of pensioners. Neat as grandma's parlour. A deep, gentle voice. None of the signs of letting go you sometimes see in retired people. He wasn't sitting unshaven in his bathrobe. But he could have been any proud, elderly man. Except for the cats.

They sat gazing at you from every corner of his large Victorian terraced house. If you had a guilty conscience they could have driven you insane, like the man in Edgar Allan Poe. Tabbies and gingers, tortoiseshells and marmalades, three-coloured cats, grey cats, white cats, black cats. Lots and lots of the black-and-whites Cat Man said you get if you let them breed the way they want to. There was a cat with one eye, a cat with one ear, a cat with three legs and at least one with no tail. They were sleeping or standing or running or walking or climbing. Mostly they just sat and stared. I make the scene sound restless and confused, but the most amazing thing was the peace.

'How do you know you haven't got other people's pets?' I asked.

'Oh, I'm sure I have,' he answered evenly. 'Most cats have two or three lairs – places where they eat and sleep anyway.

I'm a sort of clearing house for local news about cats.' I couldn't deny that. I was new in the neighbourhood, and I'd been enquiring about my kids' cat, Coconut, who'd disappeared, as cats do. 'Don't bother with a card in the shop,' people said. 'Go and see Cat Man first.' So I had. But I wasn't prepared for all this.

And I couldn't deny his inventory was spot on. I searched his labyrinthine dwelling, impressed there was no cat mess and no smell. I spotted at least three black short-hairs that might have been Coconut. However, when I told Cat Man he had five white hairs on his breast the old gent gave a sympathetic grimace and said, 'Sorry, he's not here.' And he was right. It was humbling. I thought I knew Coconut really well. 'Your cat will be back,' he said. 'Most likely he's been unsettled by your move. His friend, Tyger, is still there, you say?'

'At the moment,' I replied, my spirits sagging.

'Then he'll be back.'

I wanted to believe him, but I was afraid he was reassuring me out of kindness. Not that I cared desperately about the bloody cat. In a couple of months, though, my kids would be back from the States, and if Coconut was gone they'd be distraught. And my ex would count it as another Bad Dad mark against me. Not even up to cat-sitting.

A few days later, however, I found a cat's fang – tiny, dingy and sharp – on the stairs up to my flat, and desperate logic told me Coconut had been back. He must have come in through the cat flap, snatched something to eat and gone out again. I quickly checked Tyger to make sure it wasn't her tooth, but there was no real reason to think it was Coconut's either. Except that it was. Next day he came wandering in minus one fang, hopped on the bed, snuggled up to Tyger and fell asleep. End of emergency. He went off two or three times more, always returning a few days later. Tyger just seemed to sleep through it all, but how do I know? Maybe she was showing concern the way cats do, keeping a kind of silent vigil.

I went back to Cat Man to thank him for his good advice and let him know Coconut had returned home. The place seemed exactly the same, like the wallpaper was made of green eyes. He had a new cat you couldn't miss, a giant tiger tom he called 'Bouncer', the biggest domestic cat I've ever seen. When you walked in he trotted up and greeted you like a friendly dog. So with Bouncer purring on my lap as if he'd known me all his life, Cat Man and I got to talking over a cup of tea – he was telling me how ginger cats came over with the Vikings – and I asked him the one thing I was really curious about: how he'd become Cat Man in the first place?

He had a long sip of tea and said, 'Well, I suppose I started because my late wife was a Bird Lady.' It wasn't exactly the answer I was expecting. 'People who found distressed or injured birds brought them to her, and she'd nurse them. She was good at it too. People soon realised she was better than phoning the RSPB.'

'This is Mavis?' I asked as gently as I could, sipping the strong breakfast tea. He'd mentioned her before, always in a reverent voice that irritated me. He nodded. 'When she died I tried to keep the bird thing going, but I hadn't the gift. I've seen her put a bird down her blouse and warm it between her breasts until it recovered.'

Of course I censored my joke about blue tits, but I'm afraid the tone he adopted towards the saintly Mavis brought out the adolescent in me. It was in complete contrast to the down-to-earth way he talked about the cats.

'It isn't something you can acquire. I kept the feeders going, but people stopped bringing me birds.' He sighed heavily. 'My daughter, Phoebe, has her mother's talent and her love of birds, so at least one of us in the family continues the good work.'

'So where is Phoebe?' I asked, shifting under the dead weight of Bouncer, trying to get some feeling into my bottom. 'Not next door, I hope?' I pictured his moggies going over the wall to feast on Phoebe's little feathered darlings.

'Oh, no, she lives down south. She has a family. I seldom see her.' He said it in a falsely casual way that made it sound really important.

He took another long sip, set his cup down and stared into space. For a moment I wondered if he'd gone to sleep. Then he spoke. 'One day a cat turned up. You won't believe this, but there was a knock on the front door – I remember distinctly someone banged on the knocker three times – and when I opened the door there was no one there except a small, three-coloured cat, black and white and orange. Three-coloureds are always female and supposed to bring you good luck. At first I thought she was a kitten about six months old – her foot pads were so soft and pink – but she never got any bigger.'

'Is she still here somewhere?' I asked.

'No, I haven't seen her for years.' He answered in the same unconvincing, off-hand way he'd referred to his daughter. 'One day she got a bird. I saw her in the shrubbery at the bottom of the garden, dragging it by one wing. A wood pigeon as big as she was. I chased her and got it off her, but it was too far gone. I remember the white slash on its shoulder smeared with blood.'

As he told this anecdote his mellow voice broke and became thin and wavering. I tried to think of something soothing to say. Bouncer was purring like an outboard motor. 'All your work with your wife,' I said. 'You must have been used to dying birds.' I waited while he drank tea, cleared his throat and collected himself.

'Yes,' he said, his voice level again. 'I was the one who had to wring their necks when they were beyond hope.' He shook his head, and I felt I'd put my foot in it again. 'I still don't understand why it upset me so, this incident,' he said hoarsely. 'I suppose I felt responsible. Like I was giving out mixed signals by keeping a cat. But instead of getting rid of the cat, I gave up the birds. It was hard. I'd had so many hours of pleasure watching them feed. Especially when it got cold and they came in from the woods. I had greenfinches and redwings and even the odd goldfinch.'

'It sounds lovely,' I said, deciding to back off and ask no more questions.

'Then almost unconsciously I started with the cats,' he went on. 'Feeding strays, taking in boarders. Running up a bill at the vets.'

'Why not just get your own cat?' I asked.

'Yes, why not?' He smiled and shrugged. 'I never pictured it like this. Living on Planet Cat. Once a week they clear out when I Hoover. Even then the deaf ones sleep through it. My grandchildren love coming here – they just love all the cats. But my daughter hates it. I've become a sort of family joke.'

Then Bouncer sat up as if someone had stuck him with a

pin. He looked around the room, turning his big head slowly, peering at me through slit eyes. I was a little scared he might be going to attack. It would be like fighting a bale of razor wire. Instead he put his great paws on my chest and started licking my face.

Cat Man laughed and said, 'He loves the salt.' I said I had to go.

'Bouncer really likes you, and I can tell you why. It's because you remind him of the little three-coloured cat, who was my wife.'

'Your wife?' I stopped breathing.

'Yes, she was Mavis. I could tell by the way she walked, and the way she held herself.'

I wanted to ask how you compared a four-legged walk with a two-legged walk, but we seemed to have gone beyond all that. And who was I to criticise his grief for his wife? Even by implication. Most of the world needed to believe in some form of life after death.

I walked around the front of the house and I looked at the upstairs window, wondering if I'd see ten or twenty pairs of eyes staring down at me. Cat Man had said he kept two rooms upstairs cat-free, his bedroom and a guest room. Only one pair of eyes gazed down, a green pair, from a single window at the very top of the house. They belonged to a small, three-coloured cat, black and white and orange.

She put her paws on the glass and stretched, showing her pink pads and white belly.

FRED

She woke miserable and lay there unable to move. Fred came into the room, circled the bed and gave her his most soulful look. He put his paws on the sheets. She told him to get down. Then he sat back panting, thumped his tail on the floor and exuded hope and good cheer. Walkies. Would she be able to face a walk this morning? She ought to go out. It would do her good, get all those beneficent body fluids moving. At least Fred still loved her.

If only she could rewind her life video twenty-four hours and start yesterday all over again. Where was Glen? The space beside her in the bed seemed vast. These days he always waited in bed, waited for her to bring him breakfast. Had he gone in to the spare room to sleep? What if he was still raging? Last night she'd thought he was about to attack her. When she said she didn't feel guilty, and he said she bloody well ought to, he picked up a hardback copy of *War and Peace* as if he was going to hit her. Instead he stuffed it into the wardrobe drawer with the socks. He still obsessively tidied things away, as he'd always done, but now he never remembered where anything went. She found the mustard in the bathroom cabinet, her glasses in the dustbin. She really should get up and look for him. He could be stuck in the bath again. He could have fallen.

But she was helpless to move. She might as well be super-glued to the sheets. Fred gave a groan of resignation and hit the floor with a thud. She looked at him. He was an old dog, but his smoky-grey coat was still handsome. It was soothing to lie and stroke his warm fur. And he was content so long as she was touching him. Maybe she'd just keep her hand on him and go back to sleep. Except she had to look for Glen.

'Fred,' she said, 'where's Glen? Find him, boy.' Fred sat up, panted some more, looking hopeful, then laid down with another thump and moan.

She wasn't sure she could face Glen's anger again. In all their thirty-six years together, she'd never seen him so furious. She wasn't sorry she'd had sex with Taylor. She needed it, and so had he. It was a good memory already and would continue to be. The swim together. The bottle of plonk in front of the wood fire. Making love on the scratchy rug. A bit nervous and tentative, but lovely. It was good with Glen too. Still good. Why had she been seized with a fit of honesty and confessed?

She knew it wasn't the sex she needed. It was the company, the intimacy. Taylor needed it as well. He'd put a brave face on his divorce, but she knew it had cost him a lot more than the money. She still had Glen, yes, but that was a little like saying she still had Fred. A cruel thought, but true. She had the years of loneliness to prove it. Claustrophobic years. There couldn't be that closeness with someone whose brain was running down like an old battery. Not even with Glen, whom she loved more than anything. She knew about her honesty too. Still getting her into trouble. Her confession, blurted out after they'd started talking in bed – that was an attempt to be close to Glen, a clumsy grab for nearness. The kind everyone can do without.

It hadn't been fair to Taylor either, telling Glen before they'd even discussed it. Glen had shouted he was going to murder Taylor, but she couldn't take that seriously. She thought of Taylor's plump body and rolled over to face the wall. Fred was squeezed into the space between wall and bed, licking her hand. He smelled of bacon. Maybe Glen had been feeding him.

Then the phone went and she heard Glen answer. Shit, shit, shit, she said out loud. He did this all the time. The answer phone was always on, yet he insisted on answering. He still could take a message, but by the time he got upstairs he'd usually forgotten it. If some well-meaning person tried to strike up a conversation, he lost the thread and hung up. Sometimes he just picked up the phone and hung up without answering. She could hear him talking, quite a lengthy chat for him.

Now he was climbing the stairs. She braced herself, wondering if they would ever recover from this. Would he say he forgave her but still bear a grudge, like so many couples she knew? She couldn't leave him. That was out of the question. Why were the stairs taking him so long? He'd always been heavy-footed, but now every creak sounded ominous.

He walked into the bedroom smiling, carrying a breakfast tray. Fred jumped up, his tail hammering the side of the bed. 'Darling, that was Taylor. He wants a swim. You go if you want to, all right? I don't feel up to it.' Humming a tune, he set the tray on the bed. A bowl with dog biscuits in milk.

'What did he have to say?' she asked.

'Nothing. Just that he wanted a swim. I don't feel up to it.' He started tidying the bedside table. She'd have to check the bins later.

'You were chatting away with him,' she said.

'Are you going to church?' he asked.

'Would you like to?' she said. 'It's Saturday, but we could go tomorrow.'

'I don't feel up to it,' he said again.

'What about last night, love?' she asked, steeling herself. 'You need to talk about it?' She couldn't believe he'd forgot.

'Last night? You mean the film?' They hadn't been to a film in weeks.

Now he was tidying the dressing table. 'Where's Uncle Jim?' he asked. 'He's not in his room.' Uncle Jim had died twenty years before. Glen missed him a lot.

'Maybe he's gone for a walk.' She gestured toward the bowl. 'Is that for me?'

'No.' He looked at her as if she'd gone soft in the head. 'It's for Fred. Here, boy.' He put the bowl on the floor, and she watched Fred fall on it like there was no tomorrow.

'Love, are you sure you don't want to discuss last night? You were so upset.'

'Was I?' he said. 'What, did you leave the back door unlocked again?' 'Never mind,' she said. Fred was making loud lapping and crunching noises. She started to chuckle. 'I thought I'd make you breakfast,' announced Glen. 'Guess what it's going to be?'

'Well, I smell bacon,' she answered, playing the game.

'In New York,' he said, 'they call it an Irish breakfast, and in Ireland they call it an English breakfast, but in Wales they call it bacon and egg.' One of his favourite jokes. She heard it nearly every morning.

'And toast too?' she said. 'With butter and homemade marmalade?'

'Absolutely,' he said. For a moment she wondered if he could actually do it.

'I don't want a swim today,' she said, sitting up and putting her feet in slip-ons. 'I just want to be home. I'll come down and give you a hand, then we'll take the dog for a walk.'

PERRY

Flo looked up from the blank page in front of her, and there among the green leaves of her Williams pear tree was the most beautiful bird she had ever seen. It was small like a finch and bright butter yellow all over. Suddenly it sang and Flo felt the notes to be as golden as its plumage. Still rapt in wonder, she slowly became aware that this spectacle was nothing more than a common canary, the sort you see in cages and never look at twice. But the sight of it here, among the fat yellow pears in her own tree in her own garden, the surprise of seeing it as a wild thing among the leaves and flowers, made her view it with different eyes. For a moment she understood why people coveted canaries, wanting to keep them in cages – something Flo regarded as a barbaric practice.

Then, almost as if the canary wanted to prove to Flo it was no mere beast of nature, it did something a wild bird would never do. It flew to the open door of her conservatory, rested a moment on the steps, then hopped inside. Flo knew it was important to recapture it, that a house bird would never survive in the garden. The tits using her feeder would surely peck it to death, if the neighbours' cat didn't get it first. She tiptoed to the conservatory door and shut it softly. She glanced again at the bird, perched on a hanging basket and singing its

23

heart out, then slipped through the house and closed the French doors to the living room. It was now trapped inside Flo's glass prison.

Flo earned her living as a writer, and was glad to be distracted from the terrible tedium of her blank page. She went round to the local pet shop and put a card in the window. 'Found, one canary.'

Just going into the shop was a bit of an ordeal. She tried not to look at the cages. There were incredible budgies striped like zebras, canaries that looked like they'd been dusted with cinnamon. And there was one particularly lovely canary, a rich yellow like the one she'd just captured, but with a drift of white on its wing, as though it had recently brushed against fresh paint. It was busy chewing its metal bars and scratching a tatty sign that said 'Fifi'. The proprietor recommended Flo contact Citizens Advice and the police, both did lost pets. Oddly enough, it was the police who seemed most interested. They said they'd contact someone. Didn't they have anything better to do, she wondered, like catching the burglar who broke into her house last Christmas?

In less than half an hour Flo's front doorbell went, and when she opened the door, she was staggered. There on her front step was the most gorgeous, dashing young man she had ever seen outside the movies. It was all she could do to prevent her eyes going out on stalks and her tongue hitting the floor. He laughed as if he knew the effect he was having. 'I hear you've got my Perry,' he said and waved a large wooden cage. 'I'll take him home before he makes a mess.' Flo invited him in, struggling to hold on to her composure. She chattered away, unaware of what she was saying. She knew she was doing a lot of simpering and giggling, and once she even snorted like a pig. Eventually the young man closed the door of the conservatory, and Flo waited for the scramble, hoping he wouldn't break anything. Instead he simply placed his cage on a table beside a pot of glossy basil, opened the cage door, sat down in a wicker chair, crossed his long legs and smiled at Flo. His smile was brilliant, very white against his very black skin, and when he smiled his black eyes flashed. He was dressed in loose linen, beigy whites all over, and white shoes. Flo realised she was staring and started miming having a cup of tea – would he like a cup of tea – but he laughed again and shook his head. Just then the bird flickered to the table, hopped into the cage and started to feed. He shut the door. That was it. While Flo was still wondering how she would keep him there for a chat, he was out the door and down the road. After he had gone she thought of a hundred clever gambits. How would she manage to meet him again, other than doing sad things such as hanging around shops where they sold bird seed?

A few weeks later a gang of roofers came to the door and said her roof needed mending. Still with her mind on the beastly blank page, which now had a lot of pointless words on it, she believed them. They got their ladders off the van and went up on the roof and did a lot of hammering. Then Flo gave them a cheque, and they went. The cheque was so large, however, she began to have misgivings and rang her friend, Jeremy, who came round after he'd finished at the office.

'You've been ripped off,' declared Jeremy after he'd listened to her story and walked around the house craning his long neck. 'You, not your shingles. The shingles appear untouched.'

'But they went up ladders and did all that banging,' protested Flo. 'They had stacks of shingles.'

'Pure show business,' said Jeremy. 'Don't you know tricksters like that prey on single women?'

'No, they were genuine. I'm sure of it,' she said.

'Of course you are,' he said. 'Con men are more convincing than the real thing. Don't you remember you had the roof done last year?'

Flo sighed heavily and shook her head. 'Phone the bank,' he said. 'They won't get away with this.'

Flo hadn't the confidence to argue. Jeremy rang the emergency number and got the payment stopped, apologising for the naivety of his friend, who was obliged to come to the phone and confirm her stupidity. The girl at the bank even had the cheek to laugh at the name on the payment – 'Reliable Roofing'. To make Flo's humiliation complete, Jeremy called the police. She said the police would be useless, but he insisted. These men were on the wrong side of the law. Jeremy was in an ecstasy of omniscience.

Once Sergeant Holmes saw that name and address on the phone message he had only one thought, to meet again Ms Florence Ridgeway, the beautiful older woman who had rescued his bird, Perry. After he'd got Perry home that day he cursed his habitual shyness. Now he had another chance. His mate, Steve, said it was a man who phoned. Maybe she was married or had a partner. He could have sworn she lived on her own. His trained eye had seen no sign of a man in the house. So much for the deductions of Sherlock.

He knew the cowboy roofers. They weren't from the area, but every now and then they descended like hill bandits. The office had a thick file of statements attached to 'Reliable Roofing' invoices. Their business address was invariably a fake and the telephone number unobtainable. Probably they operated from a pub somewhere. They wouldn't have a bank account either. They'd simply sell their cheques for a fraction of their face value to a dealer, who would then try to clear them through some dodgy account.

Steve started teasing him about Ms Ridgeway, laughing his mad laugh. Steve wasn't the nudge-and-wink sort, more the elbow-in-your-ribs-and-laugh-like-a-trip-hammer sort. Steve was the one who'd taken her call about Perry and rung Holmes, knowing he'd lost one of his birds. 'What a saddo' was Steve's comment when Holmes told him about his flying visit to the delectable Florence. 'Not only did you fail to chat her up,' he said. 'You failed to let her chat *you* up.'

As Holmes drove round to her house his breath got shorter. He wondered if his attraction to Ms Ridgeway was somehow racist. She was such a pure Nordic type. Strong beautifully boned face. Ice-blue eyes. Not a bottle blonde, but almost completely lacking in pigment. He didn't need Steve to warn him that this time things would be different. Now he was a cop. In uniform. People were funny about that. It might be OK calling round in mufti, but what about blue serge and brass?

The door was answered by a man who looked about ten feet tall and introduced himself as Mr Guy.

'Is this your house, Mr Guy?' asked Holmes.

'What's that got to do with anything?' said Jeremy, who'd had a sod of a day at the office. 'It's my friend, Ms Ridgeway. She's been swindled, and I made the complaint in her name three days ago.'

'Just trying to establish the facts, sir,' said Holmes, smiling to himself and filling in a form on his clipboard. 'Perhaps I should speak to Ms Ridgeway.' Good on you for calling the Bill, thought Holmes. He wondered why the divine Florence had anything to do with this twit. Did she run a basketball team?

The goddess herself was clothed in complementary shades of green and seated in her conservatory amid thick flowers and foliage.

'Oh, it's you!' she said, jumping up, then sitting down again. She looked like she wanted to embrace him, making Holmes feel considerably taller than Mr Guy. Slam, dunk.

'Yes, you found my bird,' he said. 'I thought maybe this was the same house.' Holmes wondered if she noticed what a crap liar he was.

'You're a policeman!' she exclaimed, as if she'd only just noticed. 'Your tailor's done a good job.' She stood up again to admire his uniform and finger the buttons.

Flo told her canary anecdote to Jeremy, who listened coldly and looked at Holmes as if he was wearing fancy dress, and wasn't a proper policeman at all. He seemed to take it as a personal affront that Sgt. Holmes and Ms Ridgeway had already met.

'How is little Perry?' asked Flo. 'I hope he hasn't been on any more flyabouts?'

It was Holmes' turn to simper and giggle. 'Perry's got a friend now, Fifi. He's more than glad to stay home.'

'I'm afraid I haven't got long,' said Jeremy, jerking his arm and doing some blatant watch-checking. 'Sergeant, have you heard of "Reliable Roofing"?'

'Oh, you run along if you have to, Jeremy. I'll take care of this,' said Flo.

'I wouldn't think of it,' he said. 'Sergeant?'

They quickly got through the 'Reliable Roofing' business, and Holmes left his card, urging Ms Ridgeway to phone him if she heard anything more, promising the cowboy roofers would be caught sooner or later. Mr Guy gave a sceptical snort.

Taking Steve's advice Holmes waited a few days, then phoned and asked if Ms Ridgeway would kindly come to the station and look at a few mug shots. When she arrived she was greeted by Steve, grinning behind the bullet-proof glass. Flo wondered if he was on pot or something. He seemed to titter at everything she said.

Before long the splendid Sergeant Holmes emerged in his uniform. He took her down a long hallway to a small room that contained nothing but a video player, a monitor and a couple of chairs. Everyone she passed seemed terribly friendly. She had expected Holmes to be smooth and confident in his own territory, but he seemed even less easy than before. Talking her through videos of mug shots, he kept stumbling over his words. It was all rather sweet.

'This is horrible!' she exclaimed finally.

'What is it?' asked Holmes. 'Do you recognise someone?'

'These people! I see some of them around town. They're criminals!'

'I'm afraid they look just like you and me,' said Holmes. 'A few more tattoos maybe.'

Holmes felt a complete fraud. Steve knew they had no pictures that were likely to be 'Reliable Roofing', so he'd dug out photos of the usual suspects, burglars and pickpockets. Holmes wished he hadn't done it now. Flo looked so lovely. She'd made a bit of an effort, though not too much. She wore a filmy net thing over linen trousers and a teasing silky shirt.

'Oh, my God!' she shouted.

'What?' said Holmes. 'Is it a roofer?'

'It's my window cleaner! He's a burglar!'

'Oh yes, Red Carter. Well, he was, but...'

'I had a burglary last Christmas. Could it be him?'

'Did you report it?' asked Holmes.

'Jeremy did. Mr Guy. The police came round and the fingerprint man left the most terrible mess.'

'I'll cross-check the prints again,' said Holmes, wondering if anyone had checked them in the first place. 'I doubt if it's him. At Christmas, I suppose it's possible. He's got a cider habit, and looks after the kids on his own.'

'I hope it's not,' said Flo. 'I like him, and he's a good window cleaner.'

Holmes was glad when it was all over. He took her back to reception wondering if he'd have the courage to say what he'd planned.

'Please do check about the burglary,' said Flo, trying to ignore the silly man waving behind the glass. 'It still gives me nightmares. I know there's not much you can do, but I'd feel a lot better if you'd just have a look at the file.' She wasn't going to leave without having an excuse for contacting Holmes again. She wondered what his first name was.

'I'll be glad to,' he said. 'I'll be glad to,' he repeated. They stood looking at each other. 'I wonder if you'd be interested in seeing my birds sometime,' Holmes said, finally getting the words out. 'You know, Fifi and Perry. And the rest. They're very pretty. I have a proper aviary.'

'I'd be delighted,' said Flo, not being able to believe she was actually going to look at birds in a cage. They made a date for her to drop round, and Flo wondered if she should tell Jeremy. She decided she wouldn't.

PURSE

She grabbed my wrist and held so tight it hurt while she checked her bag to see if anything was missing. Meanwhile I stood there rigid as a plaster saint. She was a thin, pale young woman with a surprisingly strong grip. We were at the zoo, pressed into a small crowd of people watching Ellie the Elephant eat her lunch. One of Ellie's tricks was to lift things like sandwiches out of people's pockets and bags. She'd just snatched my apple when I wasn't looking. Elephants look so gentle and distracted, you don't expect one suddenly to grab the food out of your hand. And now people were gaping at us rather than Ellie, me and this strange young woman locked together. She searched her bag and finally drew out a small black leather purse and checked the contents. Then she released my hand – threw it away rather. Still facing me, she backed off to the other side of the enclosure and stood staring. I'm sure half the people there thought I was a pickpocket. How could I point to the elephant and say, 'It's not me, it's her!'?

I turned around to leave, and there blocking my way in front of the iron gate was the young woman who'd grabbed my wrist. I didn't have time to wonder if I was going mad. I turned again and there she was, staring at me from the other side of the crowd. I repeated this turning and looking until I was certain: identical twins, identically dressed, black leggings and jackets, and carrying black canvas bags. I felt a buzzing and hot feeling around my head, as if I had a faulty electric circuit in there.

Then they started following me around the zoo. I met Mary in the cafeteria, as we'd arranged, and attempted to ignore them. When Mary finally asked me what was wrong I tried to explain. It sounded so ridiculous and unreal. The twins were there as evidence, sitting at a table near the door, but evidence of what? No doubt they'd be thinking Mary was my accomplice. I looked at her. No one could have looked less like a sneak thief. She appeared to be dressed for church. But how did I know? Maybe that's the way thieves dress these days – the camouflage of the conventional. In the end Mary took charge and suggested we go, so we did. We left the zoo. And we hadn't even seen the giant fruit bats.

An hour later I was feeling much better. The twins hadn't followed us, and Mary and I were chatting and drinking scrumpy in a cider pub not far from the zoo. The pub was quiet and uncrowded for a Sunday afternoon. By now Mary was convinced my stupid Ellie the Elephant story was true, and I was relieved just to have her believe me. I hadn't known Mary long, but I felt she was trusting and trustworthy, and that meant a lot to me.

We'd changed the subject and were talking about trouble with Mary's car when a woman directly in front of us stood up and let out a howl. She started ranting to the woman sitting next to her, then picked up her bag and strode to the bar, where there was more commotion. Her friend sat looking uncomfortable for a moment, then followed her. Next they were both marching in our direction. The one making the row was as broad as she was tall and had a voice like a cattle auctioneer. She announced that her wallet was missing and asked if we'd seen anyone near their seats. We were certain we hadn't. We sat facing their table only a few feet away. 'Besides,' said Mary, 'I'm sure you took your bag with you when you went to the bar. Was your wallet inside?' The woman thanked us brusquely, turned away and continued to rummage mechanically in her bag. Her friend then stepped up, towering over us like a prop forward, gave us a suspicious look and asked again if we'd seen anybody. 'Perhaps something happened at the bar,' I said, my voice squeaking. It's weird how people can make you feel guilty, whether or not you've done anything. 'I think I'd better go home and go to bed,' I mumbled to Mary when they'd gone back to the bar for another altercation. 'This just isn't my day.'

'If we go now they'll think we're thieves,' she said. 'Besides, I'd like another half of scrumpy. Watch my bag while I go to the loo.' And off she went. Mary was nothing if not practical. It was another thing I liked about her.

Then it started again. The hot feeling around my head. The prickling up my back. The buzzing. Staring straight ahead, I slowly tipped Mary's bag on its side, unzipped it and winkled the little purse out so I could have a quick look. A wad of tenners. I only took one, knowing she wouldn't notice, and a packet of tissues. I hoped that would be enough. I was munching bits of scrumpy when Mary returned, settled beside me and gave me her warm, reassuring smile.

DANCING BEAR

Ben sat at the kitchen table and stared at the music box. It was made of cardboard painted in bright colours, and at the base was a drawer with a tiny brass knob. Behind a plastic window stood a jolly, pot-bellied bear holding up its arms ready to dance. Ben wound the key and a tune tinkled. The bear started to jerk and shudder. One arm dropped and went up again. Its legs waved in stuttering movements. Maybe it needed some oil.

Ben wondered whether he should put it back in the rubbish. He recalled the only dancing bear he'd ever seen in real life, glimpsed from a bus in Istanbul, a small brown bear on a heavy chain. It had sores on its neck. He got up, walked into the backyard and admired the results of his clear-out. Lined against the wall were green bags for recycling, blue bags for charity shops and black bags for total garbage. Earlier he'd stood there surrounded by his tidy display of flowers and culinary herbs, holding the music box in his hand and vacillating about whether to get rid of it. He hadn't forgot the day Jessie bought it for him, in a moment of silliness. Now she lived in Australia. She had a family – a husband, children. And today he was in a throwaway mood. It was such a relief getting shot of all this junk. Casually he'd chucked the box in a black bag and gone on with his work. Later he was moving bags against the wall when abruptly he heard the tune – faint, tinkling from deep inside one of the bags. He stood for a few long moments staring at nothing. Then he tore open the bag, dug down through the cold slime of potato peelings until he grasped the box and drew it out.

Ben left the music box on the kitchen table and set about making himself one of his favourite meals – fresh pasta with sage from a pot in the yard and olive oil he'd brought from Italy. After lunch he went back to contemplating the box, his attention wandering to the little drawer with the brass knob. He couldn't remember the drawer. How long ago was it, that day shopping with Jessie? Ten, fifteen years? He tugged on the knob. The drawer stuck, then gave way and opened.

Inside were three things. The first was a pebble from the beach, the sort of stone that you varnish because it looks pretty when wet. This one was dry and dull, but the memory it conjured up was not, a day at the beach with Jessie. They'd got lost on a walk, and the tide had come in and swept away most of their things, including his camera and Jessie's watch. It was the kind of day that inspires so much bad poetry about souls touching. Ben had written some himself. Thankfully it had gone out with the trash long ago.

The second item was a piece of grey card with handwriting on it, Jessie's writing. It said 'Jack Boots for Ghost of the Gestapo', 'Plaited Wig for Viking Vandal'. He remembered the play, one of his own scripts – an updating of Ibsen's *Peer Gynt* which he had thought pretty good. The production was a struggle, though, with the director disappearing two weeks before opening, then reappearing a month later as if nothing had happened. Jessie helped with the costumes and did a great job, plenty of flair and no fuss. At the time their relationship seemed solid. Before she upped and went.

The third thing was a small, blood-encrusted tampon, from the first time they made love, during a walk in the bluebell woods which became one of their special places. Ben could remember carefully withdrawing the tampon and gently easing himself into Jessie, who smiled up at him. All around where they lay were beech trees, and under the beeches there was no undergrowth except the bluebells, millions of them. They seemed to hum the colour blue like a holy chorus. Ben stared at the small cotton cylinder and tried to remember how it felt to love someone like that. He couldn't. He knew he hadn't felt it since.

Slowly he replaced the three items in the drawer and shut it. The box gave a few pings. He sat for a long time dreaming, gazing at the bear. When the phone rang he started as if asleep. And it was only after he hung up, still half in a trance, that he appreciated the joke. A person from Porlock had phoned. Interrupting his dream. Not someone he owed money, but a bookseller who had a book on cricket he'd been searching for. Ben went upstairs to his study. From his neat files he pulled out a box full of cards from last Christmas. He looked at one of the cards and slowly exhaled. It was uncanny. Jessie's card had a jolly bear on it. Why? They'd never had a thing about bears. Pigs, yes, and chickens, but never bears. He sat down at his computer and typed in his password. That was weird too. It was EISSEJ – he'd put that in a couple of months before, just for the fun of it. This must be fate, he thought, or at least heavy plotting. He typed in the email address from her Christmas card and began: 'Hi, Jessie! Greetings, from the planet *RAEB*. Bet you thought I was dead.'

LOVE RAT

He likes to watch them make love, though being a virgin he may have only a dim understanding of what they are doing. He knows he wants to be near his mistress and her divine smell. When she has sex her aroma is different, stronger and richer. He sits on top of the pine chest by her bedside, his white whiskers flicking and long white tail twitching in excitement, his pink eyes gleaming while she mates with her man.

It is dangerous to go onto the bed with the giant humans thrashing around. More than once he has come close to being crushed. But he knows his mistress would never hurt him on purpose. The one certainty in his life is her; he knows she loves him, that she is great and powerful and will always care for him. Today Love Rat is watching them from his favourite vantage point, perched on top of a thick hardback copy of *The Bedside Companion to Sex*. He is squeezed between the polished, stainless steel tube of her vibrator and the warmth of her lover's mobile phone; the vibrator is chilly but holds wonderfully its odour of her; the phone can be frightening when it suddenly rings, but is pretty and shiny and has a fun flashing red light. She is talking today, and he likes it best if she speaks while they do it. He loves her voice, to his delicate ears so deep and melodious.

'Dirty, dirty, dirty,' she is saying. 'Do it fast and filthy. Hunh hunh hunh. Talk to me, you corpse!'

'I'm talking,' he whimpers.

'You're not saying anything,' she gasps back. 'Pull it out and hold it still. That's it, just the head of it. Now move it round. Sloooowly. That's it. Now, push! Hard, hard, hard!'

And so it goes. She gives orders, and he takes them, which seems natural to the tiny rat. She is so much bigger than her lover – taller and heavier. He would have to obey.

All at once the mobile phone beside Love Rat starts speaking. Screaming rather. It makes a high-pitched, metallic, yelling noise. He is so startled he falls off the book, scrabbles down the side of the chest to the skirting board, then back up to the top of the vibrator, where he sits quivering. Her lover picks up the phone. 'Yes?' he says. 'Artie, is that you?' A voice the rat knows well and hates for its whining tone. 'What are you doing shagging Susan?'

'Peg? What did you say?'

'You heard me. Why are you porking my best friend? She's so gross.'

'What? What are you talking about?'

'Don't play innocent. I've been listening. I've even got it on tape. Put her on.'

'Pegleg wants to talk to you,' he says, offering the phone. 'She's been listening to us.'

Then she slaps him. Love Rat has never heard anything like it. He knows the sound of flesh on flesh, but not this horrible exploding noise. The phone goes flying. Love Rat leaps on the bed and scampers up Susan's back to the safe perch on her shoulder.

'That stupid, stupid phone!' she shouts. 'You have to buy one that sings and dances. She's probably got us on film as well.'

'It isn't me,' he wails. 'It's that sodding Rat. He's pressed the REDIAL button.'

'Oh yes, dumb man blames dumb animal. Why was it on in the first place?'

'He must have pressed ON as well. He probably knows how to call the vet.' Artie crawls on the carpet and finally comes up with his precious phone. He hands it to Susan, who gives it a look as if it's a dog turd, then holds it to her face and speaks.

'Hello, Peg. Artie tells me you're supplementing your desperate sex life by tuning in to us. Did we turn you on?'

'Darling, I understand someone as deeply unattractive as yourself hasn't many choices. And my husband is a sympathetic soul. His pity is easily aroused. I'm merely asking you to return him without any STIs. I don't fancy itching and scratching for the next six months.'

Susan utters a forced laugh. 'Do you ever give a speech that isn't prepared? Did you write it down as well? Look, Artie may be greasy and gruesome, but he loves me. For your sake we've kept it quiet, but if it's out now, you're the loser.' 'Put my husband on,' Peg demands.

'You think your microskirts make you irresistible,' Susan continues. 'They only make you look whorey. It's me Artie loves. Great big galumphing me. And did you know, when you cross your skinny little peglegs, you show your pants, and everybody laughs about it?'

'Hand him the phone, Susan. Or should I say "Sumo" – it's his favourite name for you.'

'And his pet name for you is "Miss Piggy"!' Susan throws the bright bit of plastic hard against the wall. Artie squeals.

'What are you doing? That cost me a hundred quid!'

'Sweetheart, pour me a brandy. We need to talk,' Susan says, unmoved.

Artie snatches Love Rat off Susan's shoulder, swings him round by his tail and dangles him at arm's length. Love Rat has never felt so exposed, hanging upside down in the middle of the room, surrounded by empty space with no place to hide. He also feels dizzy. Even worse is the acrid pong of Artie's fear, pouring off the sweat from his body.

'How would you like me to throw HIM up against the wall?' bellows Artie, and gives Love Rat a twirl.

'You hurt him even a teeny bit, and I'll never speak to you again. Never, never, never!'

'Why shouldn't I? He can't even talk. My phone can at least talk.'

'He talks to me!' shrieks Susan.

'He's a sex saboteur! This is about jealousy!'

'Artie, don't be sick. Have you forgotten all your seminars on displacement theory?'

'I'll tell you what's sick. Playing second fiddle to a rat. That's sick.'

'How can you be so pathetic? Jealous of a pet. Let him go, please,' she pleads.

Artie relents just in time, because Love Rat is near having a heart attack. He feels himself flying through the air, only to land softly on the bed. He scampers over to his mistress, and Susan feels the familiar tickle of light feet skittering up her back. He snuggles behind the hair on the nape of her neck.

Artie starts to dress in silence. The alarm goes off on his watch. It makes a piercing "skeek" noise that hurts Love Rat's ears.

'What's that for?' says Susan. 'Time to come? Or time to go?' Artie makes no reply. He is tangled up in his socks and hopping around on one foot. He barks his shin on Susan's rowing machine but makes no sound except for air hissing through clenched teeth.

'Aren't you going to say something?' says Susan. 'I do love you!'

Artie continues with his socks. His underpants are back to front and inside out.

'Talk to me!' says Susan. 'Are you frightened? You're afraid of her, aren't you? You're disgusting. Go home. Creep and crawl to Miss Piggy. Grovel like a dog. You'll know where you are with her. You give, she takes. Scared! Scared! Scared!' When Artie slams the front door she is still kneeling naked on the bed. He's even left his phone in pieces on the carpet.

Susan sings to herself softly:

Little Peg's

Got legs

Like little pegs.

Love Rat feels her shoulders shaking and goes round under her chin and down to the warm place between her big soft breasts. He has never seen her crying. He feels instinctive sympathy, but at a loss what to do. Carefully his mistress picks him up, holds him in her palm and gazes at him, weeping her colossal tears. Still shivering, Love Rat looks up at her and wiggles his nose, knowing she likes that. What he does not know is how she marvels at his coat, of a softness and whiteness to make ermine look coarse and dingy; or at the translucence of his ears, the way they seem to make a halo when the light shines through. She kisses his snout and puts him back in her cleavage, then gets up and pours herself a brandy.

A faint tinkling sound reaches her ears. It is the Bach fugue Artie has programmed on his phone. She walks over and picks up the pieces, snaps it back together and presses OK. Then she says, 'Hello?'

CAPTAIN FLINT

'I checked his anus,' said Deirdre. 'It looks OK.'

'He hasn't got an anus,' said Burt. 'He's got a little multi-functional organ called a cloaca. But yes, it looks fine. No blood.'

'Well, whatever.'

Deirdre watched as Burt inspected Captain Flint's backside. There were a lot of long green tail feathers to hold out of the way. Flint blinked and made no sound, staring at his reflection in the stainless-steel table. Deirdre thought what a fabulous old fellow he'd looked just a week ago, jade green, with wing tips of sky blue. Now look at him, his head nearly bald.

'How long's he been off his food?' Burt asked quietly.

'Only a couple of days,' she answered. 'After he started losing feathers. I'm giving him drops of dextrose.'

'He looks really well cared for, Deirdre,' he said.

She looked around the brightly lit room. Burt had set up a tidy surgery, smelling of wintergreen. In the midst of all the polished metal and white tiling the Captain made a loud explosion of colour. Burt spread his wings and examined them. Deirdre had to admire the firm but gentle way he handled her stroppy old bird. One of Burt's hands was protected by a thick white gauntlet, the other covered only by a surgical glove. The

Captain had already tried to bite him, causing Burt to launch into another of his monologues – this one about films in which people are bitten by parrots. Deirdre was amazed there were so many. The only one she knew was *The Third Man*.

'Flint's a living legend,' she said. 'He's supposed to be over two hundred years old.' She paused. 'Is that possible?'

'It has been known,' he said. 'I'd say he's more like seventy-five or a hundred. He's from the Amazon.'

'And he's supposed to know the secret of Henry Morgan's treasure,' she added.

'Which Henry Morgan, the pirate or the politician?'

'Both, for all I know. I got him from the politician's family. House clearance, after the old villain died in prison. He had a cottage here, complete with housekeeper. He used to come down on weekends.'

'While he was in jail?'

'It was one of those open prisons. Nobody wanted old Flint, so I took him as commission.'

'And regretted it ever since?' He had Flint on his back now, palpating his belly, which was a vivid Robin Hood green.

'Not for a second,' she said. 'He's been a good companion. And good for business. Customers love him.'

'The most authentic antique in the shop,' laughed Burt.

'Apart from me,' she said.

'No fishing for compliments, Deirdre. I'll only embarrass you by giving you one.'

Deirdre smiled and wished he would. She watched him closely as he circled the gleaming silvery slab. He looks a bit of a pirate himself, she thought. With his beard and gold teeth and earring. That limp. His great bulk. And she remembered the Welsh dragon tattoo on his bum, from the old days when they were lovers, both married and everything so complicated. Now he was back in the village, busy setting up his practice. Deirdre wondered if it was too soon to ask him round to Sunday lunch.

'You haven't found your Constable in the Attic, then?' he said, referring to one of their old jokes. She watched him pace to and fro. She still found that limp attractive.

'Still visit the grave, Burt? Where you buried your leg?' she asked.

'Why else would I come back to this godforsaken town,' he said. 'If not to be reunited with my leg?'

'I fancied it was me,' she said, pushing her luck.

Burt whispered, 'Watch out for this woman, Captain. She collects orphans and cripples. Heart of gold, head of brass.'

'You're not a cripple.'

'Not since I got my new leg. It's state of the art. German.' He stuck out one foot and pulled up his trouser leg, showing an expanse of dull metal. 'They guarantee you can dance the fandango.'

'No one would ever guess. You walk like you've turned your ankle a bit.' She chuckled. 'Have they left the stone? The one that says, "One foot in the grave"?'

'Of course. I'm booked into the plot myself. My only regret is they won't let me bury the motorbike.'

He gave the Captain an injection, then sat him up on the table and stroked him. Flint looked as if he'd been unplugged. Burt transferred him to Deirdre's shoulder and handed her a small brown bottle.

'Use this lotion on his head. It will ease the discomfort.'

'What's wrong?' she said. 'Is he going to be all right?'

'It's his age, Deirdre. Other than that, I'm not sure. I've got a friend, a bird specialist. I'll phone her. Then we'll see.'

'I don't care what it costs.'

'It won't cost anything,' he said. 'Maybe you can make me one of your roast dinners.'

It's a deal,' she said. 'Sunday at One?'

'OK. And I'd like to see your new pet.'

'Tillie?' She made a noise somewhere between a laugh and a squawk. 'You can't call her a pet. Where'd you hear about her?'

'If I tell you, can you keep a secret?' he said.

'Absolutely.'

'No, you can't.' He grinned. 'Nobody can in this town.'

Deirdre poured a large glass of white port, Burt's favourite after-dinner drink. The sherry and claret had been a success, and the leg of Shetland lamb was, well, something else. Burt was the sort of person who made plain his enjoyment. Going round her shop before dinner, he made noises in a selective way that hinted he had an eye for a good buy. He'd finally chosen a perfect, matt-green Denby coffee pot, the traditional style they no longer made. She hadn't allowed him to pay for it. Deirdre glanced at Burt sitting in the corner with Captain Flint on his shoulder. They looked totally at home together in the Magistretti armchair she'd stolen for a tenner from some pompous dealer in Bath. With Flint, she thought, Burt looks the complete buccaneer. All he needs is a red bandanna and a black eye patch. As if the Captain knew what she was thinking, he shouted 'Pieces of eight!' and shook his wings.

'Bloody hell,' said Burt, chortling.

'He's feeling better. It's the first he's talked for days,' she said, handing Burt his glass.

'I slipped him a steroid,' he said. 'It's bound to give him a lift for a while. Can you bring him in tomorrow lunchtime? My specialist friend is coming down.'

'That's really good of you. Of course we'll be there.'

'She's the best with birds,' he said. 'If Flint can be helped, she'll do it.'

'I don't know how to thank you,' she said, thinking she had a good idea. She wondered what his relationship was with the specialist.

'You can't improve on that leg of lamb,' he said. She looked him in the eye. He looked back. They both smiled. 'Yes, you can. You devil.' And he smiled and said, 'Are you dessert?'

'No,' she said. 'You are.' They both laughed. 'Let's not rush things, Burt. Would you like to see Tillie?'

'Yes, please,' he said, starting to get up.

'Stay there. I'll bring her in.'

'She comes in the house?'

'Every evening. She sits on my shoulder, and we watch TV. She likes the nature programmes best.'

Burt made a croaking noise. 'And she gets along with the Captain? He's not jealous?'

'The Captain loves her,' she declared.

'How do you figure that?'

'You'll see,' she said, and went out into the back garden.

Tillie was awake. Her big black eyes shone out of the white moon face. Deirdre stepped into the pen, and Tillie opened her wings and floated noiselessly onto her shoulder. There were still some dead chicks on the floor, so Deirdre knew she wasn't hungry.

When Deirdre walked into the living room with Tillie, Burt didn't utter a sound; he simply stood up, and his mouth dropped open. After a long silence the Captain started to talk rapidly in the special patois Deirdre called his Tilliespeak.

Burt sat down, not taking his eyes off the huge bird of prey. Her face was the whitest white, and the rest of her plumage a rich caramel. 'Where did you get her?' he asked in a hushed voice. 'She's the biggest I've ever seen.'

'She's a widow, one of a breeding pair kept by a friend of mine who's married to the forester on the estate. When her mate died I offered to look after her.'

'How do you feed her?'

'Not difficult,' she replied. 'The butchers help out. And every morning I get fresh dead chicks from the hatchery.'

'You want to make sure there's no sickness up there. In fact I can keep you posted,' said Burt. 'They've just given me a contract.' He made a face at the Captain, who was still wittering away. 'Captain, would you shut up!'

To Deirdre's surprise Flint did just that.

'What the hell is he saying?' asked Burt.

'I've no idea. It sounds like German. He never talked like that until Tillie arrived. She seems to like it.'

'Maybe it's barnowlspeak,' he said.

'Sounds more like *The Great Escape*. Something he got off the telly.'

'That's it. He's telling her how to escape.'

'Not bloody likely,' she said. 'He worships the air she flies in. He follows her around like a fledgling.'

49

'Deirdre, have you got a blank tape? I want to have a proper listen to this Flintbabble.'

When Deirdre woke the next morning in her giant brass bed she was half sorry and half relieved Burt was not in the empty space beside her. Things would be all right; it was better not to hurry them. Burt seemed to feel the same. They'd spent a sedate evening with Tillie and the Captain, watching TV and chatting about their children and exes, generally getting caught up on each other's lives. Burt left early with a tape of Flint's zany utterance, vowing to decipher it or die. Typical Burt.

But as soon as she got downstairs she felt an unnatural quiet in the house. Not that there was ever any real noise. If you listened carefully you could hear the clocks ticking in the shop; the central heating and fridge chuntered away softly, and Flint made little scratching sounds behind his black cover. She rushed over to the big bamboo cage and threw off the cloth. The Captain was dead. His wrinkled blue eyelids were closed and his lizard feet up in the air, like a dead bird in a cartoon. His human-looking tongue had slipped sideways out of his beak. She replaced the cover and went to the phone. Burt was already in his surgery.

'Burt, the Captain's dead,' she said, and burst into tears. Burt commiserated and said all the right things, offering to come round that evening. He assured her several times that his specialist friend wouldn't be inconvenienced. He'd ring and cancel her visit. Then he started saying things she couldn't understand.

'Please,' said Deirdre. 'Would you repeat that? I don't follow you. I'm sorry. I'm in a bit of a state.' And she burst into tears again.

'It can wait, Deirdre. I shouldn't have mentioned it. You've got enough to deal with at the moment.'

'No, no, you were saying something about the Captain. I want to know.'

'I put a note through your door this morning. Just make yourself a cup of tea, sit down and read the note. And please, make sure you're sitting down.' She thanked him for everything, and he promised to call round later. Then she hung up and hurried through the shop to the front door. There on the floor was one of Burt's posh cream envelopes with his so-familiar handwriting. On the front it said, 'Deirdre! Constable in the Attic?'

Deirdre hadn't forgotten Burt's gift for melodrama, so she took her time. She didn't make tea; she made some strong coffee and sat staring at the envelope propped against the Radford cruet set she'd picked up for a few pennies in Greenwich market. What about the Captain? She'd take the day off and bury him in the garden – deep, so he couldn't be dug up, and near Tillie's pen. There was that lovely strongbox in Victorian mahogany. She wondered how Tillie would take this. Perhaps it was a blessing she and Flint hadn't had time to get to know each other that well. The forester's wife said Tillie took the death of her mate hard. Deirdre got up and went out back to check on Tillie, who was flying to and fro in her pen, to and fro, not making a sound. She'd never done that before, behaving like a caged beast pacing back and forth. Perhaps the Captain had called to her in the night. Deirdre talked to her softly and did the best she could to try and calm her. She'd go to the best butcher and get some sirloin. Finally Deirdre went back in the house, let out a tremendous sigh, picked up a slim pewter letter opener and slit open the envelope. Burt's message read: 'Eureka! I fiddled with the tape for hours. What gibberish. But I'm sure I got the main message. The Captain's saying, "*Deutschebank Zurich drei sieben drei sieben*". It's possible it's the number of a Swiss bank account. I faxed a banking friend of mine in Guernsey and asked him to make discreet enquiries. Maybe old Morgan told his parrot where the treasure was buried. You're lucky I'm so attached to you, Deirdre, not to mention my leg, or I might have managed a sudden disappearance.'

Deirdre smiled and put the letter back in its envelope. Did people still say, 'Eureka'? She felt a pang as she remembered burning their old correspondence. Two bin bags full. Burt had insisted she burn it, like in a novel. She took this letter as confirmation he hadn't changed that much; he was still the Burt she knew and loved. Buried treasure. How sweet, how comic book. It might even be true.

DOWN IN THE BRACKEN

Sally was out of sight, down in the bracken. Normally I would have been worried, but what trouble could she get into in a place like this? A big old-fashioned estate in mid-Wales about the size of Hyde Park. She loved our holidays here. Loads of space to bang around and zillions of things to sniff.

I kept calling and calling, and she went on ignoring me. Eventually among the ferns I spied her fluffy white tail, standing straight up and wafting gently. Something had her full attention. I called again. The tail went on waving. I got out my bird-spotting glasses and had a look. What I saw made me feel like hurling.

Right next to her tail waggled four black hoofs on the end of four spindly grey legs. A sheep on its back. Making jerky movements, as if trying to run upside down.

Oh, bugger. My dog has savaged a sheep. The farmer will demand Sally be destroyed. I blundered down the hill in thigh-high bracken, telling myself this couldn't happen to Sally – it was totally out of character. My thoughts rocketed off in fantasies about heading straight back to our cottage, packing and disappearing to the city, where I'd refuse to reply to phone calls, faxes, email and snail mail. Maybe a long legal battle. I wasn't going to let them kill my dog.

When I arrived, though, it wasn't a fang-baring, blood-spattered beast I had to deal with, or a ewe with its guts ripped out. Sally was looking sweet as always, a little mournful with her mother's spaniel face. She was standing patiently beside the sheep, looking up at me and waiting for me to do something. Like, rescue it. She'd slipped into the role her father had been bred for. She was the sheep dog, I was the shepherd.

The ewe was helpless on her back, like a giant woolly beetle. She'd struggled so hard her thick, matted fleece had worn a hole in the ground. Every time she squirmed and wriggled she dug herself in a little deeper. The weather had been unusually dry, and she was covered with dust. Her amber eyes were frantic.

The estate did employ a real shepherd, Jeannie, whose cottage was semi-detached to mine. Sally and I ran to ask Jeannie what to do. Out back she had a pen with ewes and lambs she called 'probs', and I found her there feeding a lamb through the fence from a bottle. The lamb was browny-black and cute as a cuddly toy. As it sucked its tail racketed round.

'Why are you doing that?' I asked.

'His mother won't feed him,' said Jeannie, holding the bottle up with one hand and giving Sally a cuddle with the other.

She was a bit of a star, Jeannie. She'd won awards and appeared on telly with her dog, Blue, who was the only blue sheep dog in captivity – not a sheltie with blue eyes or a blue merle, but a true, all-over indigo. Because she was dyed. Regularly, by Jeannie. It started when Jeannie fell in love with a little white puppy about to be drowned in a sack. White puppies make useless sheep dogs. Apparently sheep are so stupid a dog looks like another sheep if it's white. The more black the better. So Jeannie hit on the blue solution.

'Why won't his mother feed him?' I asked, reaching through the fence to stroke the lamb. It felt both soft and wiry.

'Long story,' said Jeannie. 'He was adopted by a ewe that hadn't got a lamb, so naturally had no milk. When he tried to go back to his mum, she wouldn't have him. He was starving to death.'

'You mean sheep are as neurotic as people?'

'Tell me about it,' she sighed. 'What's on your mind? You and Sally look full of news.'

She laughed when I told her what Sally had sussed.

'I know that old ewe,' she declared, shaking her goldilocks. 'Serves her right. When we're shearing she runs and hides, then can't carry her fleece. Lucky you found her. She'd have died.'

'What shall I do?'

'You mean you didn't flip her over?' said Jeannie. 'Just go and do it. It'll be a help.'

I made a face. 'She looks too heavy,' I whimpered.

Jeannie gave me a look as if I'd just told her I sleep with my teddy bear, which I do. I'm about twice Jeannie's size.

So Sally and I went back up the hill with our tails between our legs – mine metaphorical, hers literal. In tune with our mood it started to drizzle. Not one of those pleasant, summer mizzles, but heavy, soaking stuff that was almost rain. I half hoped the idiot sheep would be gone, but there she was, still running in air. In a couple of hours she'd be one big mud pie.

I did as Jeannie advised and got down, remembering to

bend my knees, gripped the ewe's fleece underneath and pulled. After that she did most of the work. She sprang to her feet and was out of sight before you could say, 'Ram ewe'. I had no idea sheep could run so fast. All you saw was a wave shooting through the bracken like a school of fish.

We came across Blue sleeping in the deep bracken, tethered to a lone holly tree. I'd never seen Blue tied up before. Wondering what was wrong, I sat down beside her and said, 'Blue, where's Jeannie?' She gave her tail a polite wag and went back to sleep. Sally zig-zagged down the hill hunting sniffs. It was August and the ferns were chest high, giving off that lovely verbena smell. Sally and I were back on the estate for our holiday. The year before I'd gone abroad and put her in a kennel. I'll never do that again.

'Hope! Come get your bloody dog!' It was Jeannie's voice. What could be the matter? She never referred to Sally as 'my bloody dog', but she didn't sound angry either. I jumped up and went charging through the lacerating ferns, glad I was wearing jeans and a lumberjack shirt.

'I'm coming!' I called.

'Well I'm not!' she cried, and there was a whoop. Then I could hear a man laughing. I ran on in the direction of Jeannie's giggling voice. I could see the bracken waving in one spot, as if there was a little whirlwind.

They were both naked, Jeannie and the man. Sally was sniffing round them in a puppyish sort of way, wagging her tail and wanting to join the game, whatever it was. I recognised the man – it was Dave, who delivered cattle feed and stuff from town. His thin body was covered in dark hair, and with his goaty legs and short beard he looked like something off a

Grecian urn. His dick was hanging long and purple and slimy, I suppose because it had recently been in action.

'Tear your eyes away from Dave's cock and get your dog off us,' said Jeannie, giving Sally a shove which the dog saw as all part of the fun. Dave spouted a dirty noise that might have been a snigger. I snapped Sally on the leash and pulled her away mumbling apologies.

'Leave her with Blue by the holly and come back. Sally can guard your clothes.'

That stopped me. I studied Jeannie to see if this was a wind-up. She was still giggling, so it was hard to tell.

'I don't want to intrude,' I muttered. I still can't believe I said that. I don't want to intrude. So well brought up.

'I can guarantee Dave is safe. I checked him out,' she said nodding, not smiling now. Dave let loose an agricultural guffaw.

I looked at Jeannie. She wasn't on TV just because of Blue: she was pretty, very pretty. A perfect body, white and plump, with little poached-egg breasts and a blond bush as tiny as a wren's nest. What a contrast I'd be when I released my giant mammaries from my sports bra. And I was taller than Dave. When you're a big woman, you know size matters. I imagined Dave and me going head-to-head, getting a prick in my mouth and a crick in my neck. I said no, backing off, dragging Sally away.

'Come on,' she said. 'This is just a friendly fuck. Dave and I thought we'd have a go. I know he isn't much, but there's not a lot of choice around here unless you're into animals.'

Dave haw-hawed again.

I said no, thanks, courteously retreating. Next morning I

was sorry. I'm not good at being spontaneous – it's something you have to practice. Having sex with Dave, though, might have been a small price to pay for maybe getting something going with Jeannie.

There's nothing worse than the sound of a dogfight, especially if it's your dog. Like catfights, they're usually just noise – they can make a ferocious racket and do little damage. I knew Sally could hold her own against any farm dog, but I was still scared, sprinting insanely through the bracken toward the uproar, hoping she'd be OK.

As I ran I thought, I'm not dressed for this, in skimpy shorts and a flimsy t-shirt. I'm being cut to bits. It was the day after the scene with Dave. I realise now I'd put on my sexiest outfit, telling myself it was a hot day, which it was, but really hoping Jeannie would notice. I've got good legs. Maybe she liked Amazon types.

All was ominously silent by the time I got to the scene of the fight – a beaten-down circle of bracken beside a low stone wall, part of some kind of ruin. Sally and a weird-looking dog lay locked together, gasping and growling and thrashing around, neither able to get away from the other. Sally's teeth gripped tight to one of the dog's hind legs, and the dog clamped her jaws on one of Sally's.

I seized up completely. Couldn't do anything. Later Jeannie said I was standing there transfixed with a large stone in my hands. I must have had the idea of bashing the other dog's brains out and to hell with the consequences. Then, abruptly, it was all over. There was blur of indigo and a loud cracking noise, and Blue was lying in the grass proudly blinking up at me with the dog's neck in her mouth. Jeannie seemed to materialise from nowhere. She busied herself working Sally's leg free.

'It's not broken,' she announced. 'The teeth went between the leg bone and tendon. I can bandage it up, give her some shots, and she'll be fine. Are you OK?'

I believe I was perched on the wall sobbing, still holding my stone.

'Hope, don't carry on so. You'll upset the dogs.'

Jeannie took the stone out of my hand and threw it into the bracken. Then she pulled out a knife and nipped off the dog's tail. She offered it to me, but I shook my head, trying to stop crying.

'What are you doing?!' I shouted. 'Cutting off its tail!'

'I'm sorry, that's what we do in the country. Do you want her pelt?' said Jeannie. 'She's a bit old.'

'Her pelt?!' I wheezed, unable to believe my ears.

Faced with such strange urban prejudices, Jeannie went back to tending my dog. She cooed and fussed over her, finally lifting Sally up and holding her, limp and exhausted, in front of me.

'Can you carry her?' she asked quietly, and I answered of course I could, and Jeannie draped Sally over the back of my neck like a fur piece.

'Sally, you're a hero,' she declared. 'That old vixen's had more of my lambs than you've had hot dinners.'

I stared at the dead thing at my feet. There were streaks of red, but mostly it was rich brown and a lot of misty grey, even some black and white.

'You mean that's a fox?' I said, feeling a complete duh.

'What do you think it is, an alligator?'

'Her coat's so beautiful,' I blurted. 'So many colours.'

'Well it took Sally to get her,' she said. 'She must have caught her napping in the shade of the wall.'

'Isn't it amazing Sally wasn't killed? I mean, a fox?'

'A fox is no match for a good dog,' said Jeannie.

'But foxes are wild,' I protested.

'You think dogs aren't?'

'She's got a strong smell,' I said.

'She'll smell a lot stronger tomorrow. Blue, leave that.' Blue gave a look like she'd been cheated of the spoils of victory.

Jeannie knelt and ran a hand lightly up and down my bare legs.

'You're all over in cuts, Hope,' she said, stroking me. 'We've got to disinfect those. Are you up for a bit of pain?'

I nodded, smiling down at her through my tears, feeling her touch, up and down my legs, and that lovely loosening below my navel.

WHO'S THERE?

I remember I was dancing around the room brandishing my stick and practising the movements in my fresh new copy of *Everywoman's Guide to Self Defence*. The book was a 22nd birthday gift from my friend Nettie, and the stick came with it, a short, tough piece of dowelling, blunt at both ends. It wasn't classed as an offensive weapon, so you could carry it in your bag and do a lot of damage if you knew how to use it. 'Enjoy your holiday, and watch out for those Wild West Welshmen,' said Nettie laughing. I envy Nettie her laugh. I never dare laugh in that hearty, open-mouthed way, because it shows my sharp canine teeth. Of course I was called Daughter of Dracula by kids at school. Now I'm a teacher, an authority figure, I don't dare let my little darlings pick up on it, so I laugh with my mouth well shut.

There was a knock at the door. I grabbed my bag from under the bed, shoved in the stick and book and bounded over to the rocking chair by the window, where I started rocking and writing postcards. Another knock. I said, 'Yes?'

'It's Mrs Pryce, my dear. May I come in?'

It was my bed-and-breakfast lady, elderly and terribly sweet, but also a bit on the garrulous and clingy side.

'Yes, of course, come in.'

Mrs Pryce entered smiling toothily – a tall, bony, fox-faced lady, with one of those bass voices old women sometimes have. 'Just making sure you're quite comfortable and settled.'

'Yes, thanks, I'm fine.' I held my pen over a postcard.

'I hope you haven't been disturbed. I thought I heard a thumping noise. My regular residents are usually so quiet.'

'Thank you, Mrs Pryce. I haven't been disturbed at all.'

I was sure I was being told off in a wonderfully genteel way. I was surprised at the reference to other residents, though. Where were they? They had to be quiet as the dead. 'You'll probably meet them at breakfast,' she said, reading my thoughts. 'Mr and Mrs Hall, Mr Jones and Mrs McCarthy.'

'Fine.' I smiled vacuously and made body language to go back to my writing. I realised I wasn't being very nice, but I was tired from hitching and hiking and wasn't feeling chatty.

Mrs Pryce was not put off. 'I was about to walk into the village and wondered if there was anything I could get you.'

'No thank you, Mrs Pryce. That's very kind of you.'

'Oh, it's no trouble. Mr Evans has the shop beside his pub, you see, so it's easy for him to stay open late, and it's lovely to know you can pop into the village. I always buy the breakfast things fresh. Mr Evans buys direct from the farms.'

And so on and so on. No amount of looking at my watch or hinting I was knackered seemed to have any effect. I heard about the deceased Mr Pryce, who used to work for the County – roads, I think – and how she got up at six in the morning for fifty years to make his breakfast, and how she used to be a school teacher like me, and how, with both their incomes and no children, they could afford a big house like this, The Rectory, and about the history of the Rectors and what an important person the Rector was, being the one who collected tithes for the church...

I eventually ended the conversation, monologue rather, with pointed preparations for bed. It was as tactful as I could be under the circumstances. Mrs Pryce insisted on taking my cards to post. They were all in envelopes anyway, so my privacy wasn't at risk. I signed my card to Nettie, and before I put it in an envelope I looked at the picture again, a photo of a pudding-faced Welshman with a coracle on his back. I had joked to Nettie that he was the dead spit and image of one of the rapists in *Everywoman's Guide*. I handed the envelopes to Mrs Pryce, and a few minutes later I saw her walking down the drive on her way to the village. I remember thinking, how amazing, she must be in her eighties, and she's walking a mile to get my eggs and bacon for breakfast. Mine and the others – the invisible, inaudible, regular residents. And I wasn't even having bacon, since I'm vegetarian.

Mrs Pryce disappeared into the trees along some path, and I stood at the window for a long time just gazing at the view, pretty as a dream. The afternoon haze had lifted, and in the cool of the evening everything was clear and vivid. About a mile away across a tiny valley stood the village, which I can't remember the name of – one of those long Welsh words that seems to be all consonants. There was a church, with a squat stone tower topped with wood, and beside it a school – it must have been an old church school – and also a schoolmaster's house. Both the school and the house were Gothic in style, to go with the church, and were gleaming white. It seemed odd they were painted white.

I remember how I'd felt when I walked up the drive a

couple of hours earlier. The Rectory was one of those square, stone-built houses, Victorian or older, which looks full of stories and appeals to your imagination, but also seems more than a little scary. Did I really want to spend the night here? I'd been hitching all day and had only got one ride, so I really wanted to stop. I hadn't budgeted for a bed-and-breakfast – I'm trying to save for a mortgage on teacher's pay – but I was just too tired to go on. When you're hitching, the amount of energy you expend is in inverse proportion to the distance you travel. If you stand in one place all day you end up exhausted. After Mrs Pryce was out of sight I went downstairs and had a really good snoop. Nothing morbid or kinky, just natural curiosity. I wondered whether I'd bump into one of the elusive regular residents. First I went to the parlour, which contained the most fascinating collection of Victorian and Early Modern grotesque. No really awful rubbish like stuffed squirrels or cow's hoofs, but the most bizarre clutter – lamps with silky fringes, arabesque oriental vases, tables shimmering with lace, sideboards alive with bric-a-brac. It was all dusted too. The only animal-exploitation articles were a few ivory picture frames and dozens of peacock feathers ogling at you.

On a small table in a corner, arranged with velvet and silver like a shrine, stood an old photograph of a young couple. You needn't look twice to know who it was – Mr and Mrs Pryce long ago. She was lovely, tall and slender as now, and more than a little Gothic, but there was something about the look of Mr Pryce that unsettled me. It took a moment for the penny to drop: the young Mr Pryce had the same face as the man with the coracle on his back. And the rapist in my book. Was he beginning to haunt me? I quickly decided I was being stupid.

After all, it was just a clan or tribal face, a Welsh face. Lots of people looked like that, especially here.

I left the parlour and followed a passage to the back of the house, where I discovered the most beautiful old kitchen. The centrepiece was one of those huge cast-iron ranges beloved of middle-class people who pursue the rural idyll. The fire was lit, but it made the kitchen seem cosy rather than stuffy. There was a lot of beer-making equipment, which seemed incongruous. I tried to think of Mrs Pryce making and drinking her own beer. Maybe it belonged to one of the residents. The whole kitchen was amazingly neat and clean, not a speck on the brass pots and pans, nary a crumb on the quarry tiles. I suppose that was the reason I noticed a tiny bit of paper on the floor by the range, and the compulsively tidy person in me picked it up and went to throw it in the fire. Perhaps I'll never know how different things might have been if I hadn't performed this small, gratuitous act. It was a scrap of card, with writing on it that looked familiar, and when I turned it over a shock went through me as if I'd been hosed with ice-water. Looking up at me was the face of the man with the coracle on his back. I looked at the writing again, and sure enough it was mine. It was a piece of my card to Nettie, that Mrs Pryce had taken to post. Had she ripped them all up and burnt them? I lifted one of the lids and looked into the cooker but couldn't see anything except the humming fire. What on earth was going on? In seconds I went from cold shock to hot anger. But what could I do? Trash the kitchen? Wreck the place? Nothing seemed appropriate. Mrs Pryce had to be some kind of twisted person. I resolved to confront her when she came back, insist that she explain. Even nutters have to be told how they're making people feel.

The next thing I knew I was in my room breathing hard, my heart hammering like a foundry. As well as feeling angry I was starting to feel frightened. I couldn't ignore the sensation that there was no one in the house but me and Mrs Pryce. Where were those others? Should I start going around knocking on doors? This idea scared me even more. Did she keep a madman in the attic? All those silent bedrooms could house a whole company of head cases. Maybe I ought not to stand my ground and demand an explanation. Maybe I should just go.

I checked the time. Gone half past nine. Still light outside, but a bit late to start hitching or looking for another room. Would I be safe in my bed? I went over to the door and tested the lock. It worked, but no doubt the same key fitted all of the doors. By now I'd well and truly terrified myself, and I'd also begun to feel pretty foolish. I needed to keep this in proportion. It was only a postcard, after all. Maybe there was an explanation. Maybe she had a dog who chewed things. I recalled delivering Nettie's Christmas card last winter. Nettie wasn't home, and I'd poked it in the letter slot. Through the pebble-glass door I could see her dog Nicky snatch it and rip it to shreds. It annoyed me at the time, but later, telling Nettie about it, I could see the funny side. Especially when she laughed her laugh. I wished she was here now, to laugh at all this for me.

Whenever I feel hysterical or in a rage, when women are meant to scream or burst into tears, I start shouting. I just yell my head off – swearing, abuse, any anti-social language that pops into my head. I got out the *Everywoman's Guide* and started dancing around howling and waving my stick. To hell with the regular residents. In a few moments I felt heaps better. Still frightened, angry, but under control.

When I saw Mrs Pryce coming up the drive I was determined to confront her. I remembered my Assertiveness classes. I couldn't just hide and not say anything. I'd feel a coward. And the feeling would come out in some stupid way at an inappropriate time. I must remain polite. I must not shout. I must stick quietly to my point. Not be fobbed off. There might be some perfectly reasonable explanation, one I could not imagine. But I must not invent excuses for her, which I'd already started to do. I was a teacher, after all. I heard 'the dog ate my homework' sort of excuse every day from the kids. Feeling full of calm resolution, I listened for sounds of Mrs Pryce downstairs. Then I started hesitating. I couldn't make myself do it. I was still vacillating when she knocked.

'My dear,' she called through the door. 'Would you like a cup of tea or hot chocolate?'

My mouth had gone utterly dry, as if I'd been kissing deodorant.

'Come in, Mrs Pryce. I want to ask you something.' She came in.

'What is it, dear? Is there anything I can get you?'

'I want to ask you something,' I repeated. I wasn't sure my nerve would hold. My voice sounded old and reedy. I tried to keep it quiet and low, like the Assertiveness teacher said.

'Yes?' she said patiently. 'I do hope there's nothing wrong with the bath. I've only just had the plumber in.'

'I'd like you to explain this.' I handed her the fragment of postcard. 'I changed my mind about having a cup of tea,' I lied. 'I found this on the kitchen floor.'

Mrs Pryce held the tiny thing in front of her. Neither of us was breathing. Then her face just fell to bits like a little child's. She started weeping quietly and uncontrollably. I felt terrible. It was the last thing I'd expected. This aged woman with so much dignity and warmth had vanished, replaced by a little girl crying her heart out. Meanwhile the smooth, unflappable voice from Assertiveness class whispered in my ear: stop feeling guilty; you're still the injured party – this has yet to be resolved.

I took her gently by the arm and guided her into the armchair. Then I sat in the rocking chair and rocked quietly and waited. I handed her a few tissues, feeling like a brute. Finally she calmed down, blew her long Roman nose and croaked, 'It fell in the semolina pudding.'

'Pardon?' I said. It sounded so silly it had to be true.

'I'm so sorry. I truly am sorry. I posted the others. I meant to tell you at breakfast. I was so embarrassed. The cat wanted feeding before I went out. I put your cards on the shelf beside my bag, and when I turned around Alice had knocked this one into the pudding. It was all soaked and smeared. I burnt it. I don't know what came over me. I'm so ashamed.' What could I say? I patted and comforted her and said, there, there, not to worry – it was only an old postcard, everything is all right. She even confessed she'd planned to lie and say she'd lost it. Anything to conceal that moment of panic when she put it in the fire. All my fear and hysteria seemed so childish now. I took the piece of card out of her hand and threw it in the bin. My Assertiveness voice said it didn't look a bit soaked and smeared. And anyway, why tear it up? I sat on the arm of Mrs Pryce's chair and held her. Poor old woman, she felt so cold and bony. Eventually we ended our catastrophic interview.

Mrs Pryce went up to her room, and I got ready for bed, feeling numb.

'Who's there?!' I called, suddenly waking up and groping on the floor beside my bed for my self-defence stick. Like all inanimate objects it lived a perverse life of its own and had moved from where I left it. I wasn't sure what had woken me, but I thought it was the doorknob rattling, like someone was trying to get into my room. I felt frantic by the time I found the stick, which had rolled under the bed against the skirting board. Holding it straight in front of me (Don't swing it, jab it, said the Guide) I advanced through the darkness, put my ear against the door and listened. Nothing. I wouldn't want the light behind me when I opened the door, so I didn't flip the switch. I stood for a long time holding my breath and listening. Still nothing. Then I slowly turned the key in the lock. I tried to turn it noiselessly, but of course it made a loud 'pop'. Then I flung the door open and leapt into the hall, stick at the ready. Nothing and no one. The floorboards under my bare feet creaked. I turned and stepped back into the room, and there blocking my way stood the man with the coracle on his back. I mean, he actually did have a coracle, like the shell of a great Galapagos turtle. He moved swiftly towards me and threw the shell over my head. It stank like bad breath. I was suffocating.

Then I woke up. I flung the covers off and sat up in bed sweating and feeling chill. I'd been so convinced the dream was real it took some time before I had any idea where I was. I sat there wondering whether I should do the traditional things like pinching myself. Then I laid back and covered up and just enjoyed the feeling of safeness. It was all right.

I was slipping off to sleep again when I thought I heard voices. Just another dream, I told myself. But the voices kept on and grew louder. They sounded angry too. Coming from upstairs, where Mrs Pryce's room was. I held my breath and listened. A man and a woman shouting. DGSI, said my Assertiveness teacher. Don't Get Sucked In. Don't get involved. Know when NOT to assert yourself. I covered my head with a pillow and hoped it would all go away. Maybe I'd wake up again. Maybe it was a dream. Then I realised with a sick feeling that it wasn't a dream, not this time. And I couldn't just ignore it. If anything, it was getting worse. It sounded awful. Maybe poor Mrs Pryce was being murdered in her bed.

I jumped out of bed and quickly pulled on jeans and a sweatshirt. I wasn't facing this in my pyjamas. Wielding my stout stick, I mounted the stairs making as much noise as you can on a carpet with bare feet. When I got to Mrs Pryce's door the shouting had stopped. I called, 'Mrs Pryce? Are you all right?'

No answer. All was quiet.

I was sure I hadn't imagined it.

'Mrs Pryce? Please answer.'

The voices started up again. A man and a woman. The woman sounded like Mrs Pryce. It built up into the most terrible row. Something domestic, about furniture, some chairs. It was hard to make out the words, they were screaming so much. Then he started hitting her. I could hear the slaps, the blows. She was begging him to stop.

'Mrs Pryce?!' I cried out.

He just kept hitting her. She was sobbing. I tried the knob. The door was unlocked. I threw it open and lunged into the room, stick at the ready.

There was only Mrs Pryce, alone, standing by the fire gazing at me with terrible eyes. The man had apparently vanished. Where was he? Under the bed? Hiding in the cupboard like in a farce? I looked behind the door. Nothing.

'Mrs Pryce, are you all right?' I squeaked.

Then she advanced towards me and shouted at me. It's the last thing I remember. Her shouting. Only it wasn't her voice. It was the voice of the man.

I don't even remember the words. I only remember that bellowing male voice coming out of her mouth, and me standing there poleaxed, holding my stick. For all the defence it offered, it might as well have been a bunch of flowers. She must have hit me with a poker or something. Or someone hit me from behind. I don't know. I've got this ghastly crease on the side of my head. It burns, as if I've been struck with a hot iron. I don't think I fought back, even though I'm covered with bruises. I must have been dragged downstairs. The room I'm in has got to stink like the grave, but my sense of smell has switched off. Mrs Pryce brings me three good meals a day and talks to me. She talks and talks. And I have my own chemical toilet. I think she likes the company, having someone to talk to. I think that's all she wants, really. I do a lot of screaming and shouting, but no one seems to hear. The post is delivered down at the end of the drive, about fifty metres from the house. There don't seem to be any other callers, not even Mormon missionaries.

Of course I'm suspicious of the food, because of the corpses down here. I only eat what Alice will eat. Alice is my only real company, a sweet marmalade cat who squeezes under the door to hunt for mice. The others aren't company because they're

71

dead – Mr and Mrs Hall, Mr Jones and Mrs McCarthy – the regular residents. Mrs Pryce has introduced us. In varying stages of putrefaction, from the gelatinous to the desiccated, they're all sitting in a row facing the window, which is tiny, glazed with unbreakable plastic, and barred.

Mr Jones, the one nearest me, is clearly the most recent guest. He looks asleep, sitting in his nightshirt, a large balding man with a grey moustache. I find myself wondering if the moustache grew after he died, because of the walrus way it hangs over his mouth. His feet are bare like mine and totally black, as black as his face is livid. I suppose the blood, after ceasing to flow, follows gravity to the body's lowest points. I can see a bit of his bottom, where his nightshirt is rucked up, and that's black as well.

We're all locked in a spidery little cellar about fifteen feet by five. The walls are lined with shelves holding hundreds and hundreds of labelled jars of preserves – every kind of fruit and vegetable you can think of, from the exotic (mango chutney) to the mundane (stewed prunes). So ha ha I won't starve. There's only one door, solid oak and cast iron, with a gap at the bottom where I get my food. Even without the bars, the window is probably too small to squeeze through, my being a Junoesque, full-figure sort of person. If I can last a few weeks, I'll come out of this quite slim. I must try and hold on to my sanity down here. I am determined to survive.

FAY

Dave and Angela were at Karl and Judy's, helping Karl celebrate his latest promotion. Towards the end of the evening, when nearly everyone had gone, Judy's tortoiseshell cat, Fay, appeared in the living room, crawled up on Angela's lap and made herself a nest there. Dave expected his wife to shoo off the animal, but instead she sat contentedly stroking her. The only time Dave had tried to be friendly with Fay she'd hissed and spat at him. But here she was, cuddling up to Angela, licking her fingers, purring like a fan in a hot room.

Then something happened which Dave couldn't quite believe. Smiling, Angela took Fay in her arms, and the cat began to lick and suck at her right breast through the knitted jumper, kneading it with her paws like a kitten. Angela giggled and held the cat, ending up with a slimy wet spot on the chic designer number which had cost Dave more than most people pay for a holiday. At least Fay was careful with her claws. There weren't any snags in the wool.

Dave had seen Fay do this with her mistress, Judy, crawling up and down her body and rubbing her all over, much to Judy's delight and amusement. And Judy's husband Karl had a theory – indeed he had a theory about everything – that Fay believed Judy to be her mother, that they were of the same flesh and blood as well as the same species. To prove his point he would encourage Fay to lie in Judy's arms and do the thing. It became a sort of party trick – Fay licking at Judy's huge, sagging breasts. Karl thought this hilarious and endearing. It made Dave on the other hand feel disgusted – he found Judy's breasts vaguely repulsive in any case. But here was his wife, Angela, nursing this creature of darkness, giving Fay her small, pert, perfectly round breasts, which Dave felt belonged to him.

Driving home, Dave said, 'I thought you didn't like that thing with Judy's cat, the breast thing.' Angela just shrugged and laughed it off, saying maybe it was her musky perfume, that Fay was a sweet cat really. New Year's Eve at Karl and Judy's should have been a pleasant, low-key occasion. Judy and Angela had been attending classes in Latin–American cooking, so the party featured Karl's knowing selection of Chilean wines and Judy and Angela's elaborate spread of Peruvian peasant food. But Dave and Angela hadn't been getting on recently, and before the party they'd had a row about scratches on the Formica top of Angela's new kitchen.

'Please use the breadboard, dear,' Angela had said.

'I use the breadboard, Angela,' said Dave.

'Those scratches weren't made by the fairies,' said Angela.

'Are you calling me a liar?' said Dave quietly, looming. He was big and loomed a lot. 'Don't forget I paid for this kitchen.'

They arrived at the party not speaking to each other.

Later, when Dave was half-drunk because Angela had agreed to drive, he saw Fay at his wife's breast again, sucking and kneading, and no doubt purring if only you could hear over the Inca pan pipes tape. He'd just bit into a Peruvian pastry, and the contents had shot out, blistering the roof of his mouth and scalding his gullet. He went closer to Angela and watched Fay's lips work at the nipple under the eggshell-white cashmere. He could see the fangs, somehow kept carefully out of the way, and the tongue curling and flicking. The paws pushed and pushed on Angela's tight, fluid swelling, the claws out but not catching in the delicate wool.

Suddenly Dave saw red. Literally, he saw red. Capillaries in his eyes gorged with fuming blood. He lurched over Angela swearing and snatched up the cat, which bit him before he flung it across the room. Judy was furious and Karl nonplussed. Angela had never been so embarrassed. The front of her sweater looked like yesterday's spaghetti. Dave was consigned to a taxi and spent the rest of New Year's Eve at A & E waiting for tetanus and rabies shots. The dirty beast had bitten through the fleshy part of his thumb to the bone.

Later this disastrous incident was merely another episode in the history of Dave's marriage to the disastrous Angela. She and Judy were living openly as a couple in the house Judy had shared with Karl, who had run off to the Virgin Islands with his secretary.

Dave called round one sunny afternoon to talk to Angela about an awkward clause in their divorce settlement. They were sitting in the living room discussing this when Fay sauntered in, leaped onto Angela's lap and started doing the thing. Dave didn't see red again; he asked Angela politely to please get rid of the cat while they were talking. She protested Fay would only scratch at the door if put out of the room, but it was agreed she could go into the garden. When the talk had reached its unsatisfactory conclusion, Dave left the house in a state of controlled anger.

As he rounded the corner he could see Fay's intricate, many-coloured coat glowing in the sunlight. The bonnet of his Merc was covered with her tracks, where she had been soaking up the heat, and now she was curled under a nice warm tyre. Carefully Dave opened the door and, without closing it, slid quietly into the driver's seat. He did not start the engine. Instead he released the handbrake, put the gears into neutral, let up on the foot brake and allowed the big car, which was parked on a slight gradient, silently to roll.

ROACH

I don't know why I've woken up. The room is dark. On the pine floorboards there's a patch of moonlight, and in the middle is a black spot. I'm sure I can see it move. I stare and stare. Eventually, I'm in no doubt what it is. A cockroach. Pants.

I'm not a rough-it sort of person. I hate camping and hearty crap. I'm holed up in my Mum's cottage, which is really basic. I couldn't say that to her. This place is her pride and joy, but it's only one step higher than a hovel. Cockroaches would be right in line with the house style.

I've been trying to drop a boyfriend, Rob, and he started harassing me – phoning and following me and stuff – so I decided I'd disappear for a while. He doesn't *scare* me, nothing like that. He's a sweet man. He just won't give up. I'm sure he doesn't know about the cottage, lucky me.

My experience with creepy-crawlies tells me they don't come in singles. When you've got one, you've got many. I'm starting to freak out a bit, right here in bed. I had a cockroach trauma when I was six. My big brother and I were looking after a friend's pet cockroach, a giant Madagascan that lived in a glass box. It was about the size of a mouse. We kept it in our airing cupboard where it would be warm and dry. One morning I found it on my pillow. Big grey pants. I wet the bed for weeks after. My brother never confessed.

I can see the shiny armour on its back reflecting the moonlight. I know I'll have to do something. I can't just lie here till dawn. For a start I need a leak, and I don't want to let go in bed. Life in the cottage is squalid enough. In my bladder region I feel another tingle. Too much white wine with black olives, my habitual bedtime snack. I think of one night when I was sleeping with Rob and I wet the bed. He was terribly kind, comforted me and cleaned up and listened to my cockroach story. He's always kind, Rob. It gets on my nerves.

When I was at university I rented a terraced house with friends, and the very first night one of my housemates woke us up screaming. We all rushed to her room thinking assault and rape. She was crouching on top of her exercise bike pointing at the floor, where we could see nothing. Roaches! she yelled. Hundreds of them! We calmed her down and laughed at her fears, but pretty soon we found out she was right. At night you switched on a lamp and there they were, looking fat and well fed. Big grey pants, with frayed gussets. I spent a few weeks secretly wearing incontinence pads. We had a good landlord who got the exterminators. In the end they beat us, though, and we had to move out. If you brought pest controllers into one house, they simply moved down the terrace, then moved back. It was a long terrace too. You'd have had to torch the lot.

My most ghastly cockroach experience was in the south of China. I was staying with an old friend, Sue, who was teaching there. One day we had one of those tropical rainstorms that's like God has trained a gigantic fire hose on everything. Sue went into the kitchen to make us a nice comforting cup of tea, and I heard her say, 'Christ in a bucket!' in a funny voice. I ran into the kitchen. Under the sink there was no pipe, just a hole in the floor where the waste water fell through. Erupting out of the hole was a black fountain of cockroaches.

'Their drains have flooded,' she declared. Thank heaven she knew what to do and was brave enough to do it. She had a stone that fit nicely into the hole. Then she fetched a box of white powder and said, Watch out, it has arsenic in it, and started to lay down lines on the cement floor of the flat. She surrounded our beds and chairs, the kitchen table and cupboards, anywhere a cockroach might fancy contact with a human. Of course I got no sleep that night – at least it felt like it – but when I woke in the morning I could see the stuff had worked. All around the flat lay the carcasses of a cockroach army. The poison seemed to turn their insides to liquid. They'd cross the line, crawl a few more inches, then spill their guts onto the floor. One of them was a giant albino, the Moby Dick of cockroaches.

I look again. It's still there in the moonlight. I think it's moved closer to me. I need a weapon. I feel for Mum's dictionary under the bed. It's one of those serious dictionaries, weighing at least twenty pounds. I swing my feet out of bed and onto the bare boards. My toes feel so exposed. What if I step on one? I find the dictionary. Heavy reading. Picking it up, I rest it on top of my head, take deep breaths and screw up my courage.

I advance on the balls of my feet across the bare boards, holding the dictionary high. At any moment I expect a crack and squish under my foot. I think something is crawling on my heel. I stop, poise over my target. I swear it's waving its feelers at me. Silently I spread my feet wide and hold the book at eye level. Then I let go. Bam. A direct hit.

I do a tiptoe ballet to the bathroom and turn on the light. No roaches. I remember a hotel in New York where you turned on the bathroom light and there they were – tiny, acrobatic, unbelievably quick. They'd disappear down the plug hole faster than you could blink. When I found a beer can, a cheap earring and a used condom under the bed, I packed and checked out. In New York you don't spend the night riding the subway, so I ended up in a flashy place I couldn't afford.

I have a welcome pee, leave the bathroom light on like I'm two years old and creep back to bed. After the adrenaline dies down I sleep, I think. I spend hours lying there with the distinct feeling that cockroaches are crawling over my body. Thank goodness I studied psychology. I know it's a common illusion. I can't remember the name of the syndrome, though. I wake up feeling like I've been wrestling with the devil. All morning I kind of live around the book on the floor, pretending it isn't there. But it is. I haven't dreamt it all. I know that sooner or later I'll have to deal with the remains. When I lift up the dictionary and look under, there it is, partly stuck to the book, partly stuck to the floor, fragments of black skin mixed with a brown, jelly-like substance. I nearly throw up. Big grey pants with frayed gussets and sweatshop embroidery. I fetch about a hundred feet of kitchen roll and start to wipe it up without looking. I have to look a bit, to see what I'm doing, and also because I'm fascinated. When the stuff is transferred to the kitchen roll I inspect it, the way people look into their handkerchief after they blow their nose. I look again. Then I touch it. Then I taste it. Yes, I taste it. It is a black olive.

While I'm still trying to get my head round this little surprise, two more surprising things happen in quick succession. The first is, I hear a noise outside and go to the window. Pants! It's Rob coming up the path. He's wearing his naff Chairman Mao cap, which he thinks gives him a retro look, and he's swinging his stupid Wallace and Gromit rucksack. But the second surprise is, I'm glad to see him. I rush out the door to give him a big hug.

FAIREST CREATURES

Walking along the munching gravel lane between the garden cottage and the stables, Lizzie and Mark stopped and stared. Lying in the grass not twenty feet away was a horse in perfect miniature. Blinking its long lashes and looking dazed, it lay between the legs of a young bay mare who seemed to stand studying Lizzie and Mark as they ooed and ahhed.

'She looks so proud,' said Mark, wondering what the mother might make of them – two great apes with blue skins. The foal tried to rise on its thin sticks, then decided sitting was better.

'What a pretty colt,' said Lizzie. 'It looks all rusty.' She walked over toward the fence to have a closer look, but Mark hung back, wary. He watched her trying to get the mother to eat bunches of grass. Lizzie's long, coarse fair hair shone down her back. Her denims were that nice faded colour – unlike his, which were shiny new.

'From fairest creatures we desire increase,' recited Mark.

Lizzie looked over at him and smiled. 'Yes?' she said.

'Shakespeare. He wasn't talking about horses.'

'He should have been,' said Lizzie, plucking a stalk of wild grass and nibbling. 'They're the loveliest things on the planet.'

'He was talking about people. Well, a person,' he said.

'You're not getting broody again?' she teased.

'Yes, and I want you to have the baby right here, beside this barbed-wire fence. And if you feel shy you can go behind that big rock.'

'And you'll be on the other side of the valley,' she said. 'Eating grass and servicing all the other mares.'

'That's right,' he answered.

'And I'll have to bite the umbilical cord myself and lick up the afterbirth. I mean, we're talking Beauty here.' She walked over smiling and pushed him, then gave him a hug. He put his arms around her small, fit body and felt her head press against his chest. She stroked his bottom.

'Love,' she said, 'you know I'm...'

'I know,' said Mark, holding her tighter and closing his eyes. He could hear the sound of echoing water, a drain or spring underneath the road where they stood. The noise of a truck approaching made them step apart. A battered four-wheel-drive pulled up and stopped. It was towing a small covered trailer. The driver turned the vehicle round, got out and leered at them in a friendly sort of way. Mark could smell a French cigarette. Sitting in the trailer smoking was a heavyset, elderly woman who said hello to Lizzie. Lizzie went over to talk to her while the driver opened a gate and went in to the horses. Like Lizzie and Mark the driver was wearing denims, except that his were as dirty as theirs were clean. He picked up the foal like a basket of washing, carried it to the trailer and handed it to the woman, who grinned and lay it across her lap. The mare followed and was tied to the back of the trailer with a length of rope. Mark couldn't believe the matter-of-factness of it all. He half expected the mother to attack the driver when he went for her foal.

Lizzie rejoined Mark and waved goodbye as the trailer went off down the lane, the bay prancing along behind with her tail up in the air. 'She looks really proud now,' said Lizzie. 'They're taking them for a check-up. The baby's only a few hours old.'

A few minutes later Lizzie and Mark arrived at the stables. In the yard were small groups of girls in boots and riding helmets getting their ponies ready. 'Wait here,' said Lizzie. 'I'll fetch our horses.' She was quickly surrounded by a gang of girls all chattering at once. Lizzie made some comment, and the girls looked at Mark and giggled. A horse whinnied beside Mark's ear and made him jump. They all looked away, trying not to laugh. Then they disappeared into the stalls. Mark inhaled an unfamiliar smell of fresh air, creosote, urine and manure blended with straw. He was standing beside a small mountain of what looked to him like ideal garden compost. There was also the sickly-sweet aroma of sileage in black plastic bales. He was impressed with the quiet, business-like mood of the stables.

Soon Lizzie and the girls came out with a pretty black-and-white horse saddled up. 'Meet Carys,' said Lizzie. 'She's sweet and gentle. Even you will be able to ride her.' Mark watched the horse pushing and pulling at the girl who held her.

'She looks wilful to me, a bit naughty,' said Mark. 'It's breezy today,' said Lizzie. 'She gets a bit skittish when the wind is up. She'll be all right once we're out riding.' They brought out Lizzie's horse, the one she rode when she was teaching, a big black gelding who looked keen for a run.

'Carys will be fine with Black Jack,' she said. 'He won't let her do anything silly, will you, boy?' She slapped the horse's flank and nuzzled him. 'Jack, how am I going to leave you for twelve months?' She spoke softly in his ear. 'Shall I take you to Africa with me?' The horse nodded and stamped the ground.

'You can take me,' said Mark. 'I'll make myself into an instant powder, and you can just add water when you need me.' He meant to be funny, but it came out flat.

Lizzie got on Jack without saying anything, her face closed up. One of the girls handed a riding hat to Mark, and he put it on. It didn't seem to fit, so he turned it sideways and made a silly face. The girls laughed. He had several goes at climbing on Carys, but eventually he was mounted.

'You sure she likes people who can't ride?' he said.

'You can ride,' said Lizzie. 'And Carys doesn't want to spend the day kicking her heels in the stall. Come on.' And off they went, at a slow trot.

After a mile or so Mark was thinking, this is easy. Carys seemed to him a splendid little paint, the kind you see Indians riding bareback in Westerns. The last time he'd gone riding was a couple of years before, but that was little more than pony-trekking. He recalled being sore for days. Now he and Lizzie were walking the horses slowly in the bright sunshine, following a long straight ride through an evergreen forest. The most noticeable thing was the peace and quiet, thrown into relief by the knock knock of the horses' hooves and the breeze high up in the pine boughs, making a pleasantly mournful sound. 'Remember our walk last summer? To the White Horse?' he said to Lizzie's back.

'You mean the chalk horse on the hill, or the White Horse pub?'

'Both. It was the same day.'

'Was it?' said Lizzie, pulling back alongside him.

'I remember sitting in the sun high up on the hill,' he said, 'while you walked down to the horse. Just sitting and looking across the valley. I remember the London train went past, five, maybe ten miles away, this tiny train sliding along not making a sound.'

Lizzie took a drink from her water bottle. 'When I was little I used to ride that train and watch for the White Horse,' she said. 'Mum took me to London on shopping trips, and I'd look and look to see the giant horse running over the hill. I never dreamed when I was grown up I could walk there and stand on its tail. I thought it was magic.'

'It is magic,' said Mark. 'Only we've lost it. We don't know how to get it back.' Suddenly Carys started and Mark fell back on her rump, nearly coming off.

'What the hell was that?' he said in a high-pitched voice, pulling himself upright. Lizzie made little clucking noises, and her horse edged closer to Mark's.

'She's all right now,' said Lizzie, stroking the satin sheen of Jack's neck. 'One trip to London,' she went on, 'I was watching out for the horse, and all of a sudden the train passed this woman riding. She was riding fast, but the train was going faster. It was the most beautiful thing I'd ever seen. I said, "Mum, look! Can I have a horse like that?" I wanted to be the woman on the horse. I remember Mum looked so funny. She was eating a hard-boiled egg and peering out the window, this egg half in her mouth and half out.'

Just then Jack veered a little sideways and bumped Carys.

'Easy, Jack, easy,' said Lizzie. 'Stay with Carys.' Jack appeared to answer with a neigh.

'Lizzie,' said Mark abruptly. 'What am I going to do...?'

'I am coming back, love,' she said. 'It's only for a year. It's...'

'I know. The chance of a lifetime.'

'Well it is,' she said.

There was a long silence again, but to Mark it didn't seem peaceful. The pines made a moaning noise. The horses' hooves sounded like a great clock.

'Maybe it was a mistake to move in together,' he said. 'Maybe you weren't ready.'

'Don't say that. Darling...'

They rode on and gradually the rhythm restored Mark's calm. The horse felt warm between his legs. Lizzie was singing softly to herself, or maybe to Jack. Mark liked the way the pines let strong, diagonal shafts of light fall down onto the path. It was like riding along a Gothic nave.

'I was frightened last night,' he announced.

'You mean in the cottage? I thought you loved it. You're the one who wanted to stay.'

'I do love it. But I was scared too.'

'Of what?' she asked.

'Everything. It was too silent. Too dark. Smothering, like being stuffed in a sack. And things outside screaming. I'm used to the city, where there's always light and background noise.'

'Are you serious?'

'I'm scared of the horses too. Too big. Too strong. Feet like stones. Tails like whips.'

'You're impossible,' she said smiling. She kicked Jack, who let out a tremendous fart and sprang into a gallop. Lizzie and Jack disappeared up the ride.

Mark and Carys ambled along quietly for a while. He patted her neck and tried to make friendly talk, but without Jack alongside she seemed to grow restless. She kept looking around, pricking up her ears and laying them back. She stopped to chew a tuft of grass, and Mark couldn't get her to go. He felt ridiculous, like a beginner, sitting there digging his heels into her sides as she ignored him. Earlier he'd had the impression he was controlling her with his hands, but now there was no response. She'd start up running, then slow to a walk, just as it pleased her. They came to a place where there was a grove of coppiced trees with grass underneath. Carys swerved to leave the road. Mark jerked on the reins, and she bolted, galloping off. His helmet flew away. He struggled to stay mounted, the saddle thumping his body. Suddenly the horse lurched to one side and plunged down a steep embankment. Then just as suddenly she stopped, and Mark went shooting over her neck. The last thing he saw was a slab of concrete rushing towards his face.

Lizzie could hear Mark's neck break almost half a mile away. She was slowly walking Jack and thinking how she'd miss riding her favourite horse during her gap year. She hoped somehow Jack understood she'd be back. And Mark too for that matter. He was trying to be generous, but she knew he'd resent being kept in cold storage. Mark was older, though. He'd seen a lot of the world. Compared to him, she was scarcely her own person – not much more than part of other things, like her family, her job, and him.

She heard the most beautiful bird song and looked up to see a blackbird swaying on a pine bough. He was so close she could almost reach out and touch him. Then there was a distant, echoing report, and the blackbird flapped and disappeared. Lizzie thought it sounded like a rifle shot. It must be the gamekeeper culling rabbits, a pretty stupid thing to do on a day the riders were out. She resolved to register a complaint when they got back to the stables.

PATIENT

I was sitting on the No. 97 bus on my way to work. She got on at a stop beside the Castle, carrying a lot of shopping bags. She was maybe ten years older than me, in her thirties, dressed like a gypsy. A big, strong-looking woman, but not fat. Lots of long, kinky red hair. She walked towards where I was sitting, dumped her shopping on the seat just across the aisle and sat down right next to me. I started to panic, trying to keep my gaze fixed out the window. I didn't need to look around to know that, except for the driver, we were the only people on the bus. The No. 97 terminates at the Outpatients Clinic of the mental hospital. I'd heard all the stories about loonies being released to commit unspeakable acts. She opened a big brown leather bag on her lap, and I imagined her casually pulling out a butcher knife and ripping me open. I sneaked a look. As if making fun of my fears she brought out a minute pen knife, smaller than my little finger, and a dark green leaf, thick and sharply pointed. Then she slit the leaf with her knife, squeezed a liquid on her fingers and dabbed the stuff onto her lips. It was a hot day. I sensed myself starting to sweat. I could feel the cool droplets running down my ribs.

She had a strong smell, not unpleasant. Many aromas mixed together. Some kind of wood scent, and citrus, and one which was floral – but not something obvious like rose or lavender. I sneaked another look. She was wreathed in layers of dark-flowered cotton prints. Loads of freckles around her cleavage. For some reason I can't resist freckles. I could see expensive-looking sandals on long, shapely feet.

She went on staring straight ahead. I decided I'd get off at the next stop. To hell with being late for work. I hate the job anyway. I'm a security guard at a college where the Head of Security hates us guards. Hates people really. He wants to replace everybody with machines. Teaching machines, security equipment. Anything that doesn't answer back. Of course he hates students too, but hasn't figured how to run a college without them. 'Excuse me,' I said, starting to get up.

'I wonder if you could help me,' she said softly. 'I'm sorry,' I said. 'This is my stop.'

I tried to push past, but she didn't move.

'I'm getting off too,' she said, looking at the floor. 'I need help crossing the footbridge. I'd appreciate it.'

'The footbridge?' I repeated stupidly. 'Yes,' she replied. 'I have problems with traffic. Cars going past. If you just help me cross the bridge, I'll be in the park. Then it's a short walk to my house.'

She sounded so reasonable and courteous, I couldn't say no. She looked up at me and smiled faintly. She seemed familiar, but I couldn't have said why. And there was something strange about her eyes. I helped collect all her stuff, and we walked to the front of the bus. When we stood up she didn't look big of course. I'm six-foot-four and weigh about 15 stone. I felt a jerk for being frightened. I could look down on her head and see the grey in her fox-red hair. It was real red. We got off the bus and climbed the easy, gradual set of steps to the footbridge that crossed the dual carriageway. She gripped my arm all the way up the steps. I liked her touching me, but it also made me feel uneasy. I could hear her taking deep, choking breaths. I looked at her again, and my heart tightened for her as we started across the bridge. She was staring straight ahead and treading carefully. I think I felt a little of what she must have been feeling. It was like walking on a small boat. You weren't sure there was anything solid under your shoes. Not far below, tons of metal shot back and forth, and I could sense my legs going liquid, especially around the knees. If the bridge had been longer, I think I might have had to grab the railing and close my eyes. The traffic noise and smells added to a sick sensation. When we got to the end of the bridge, she was still holding on to me, but I was holding on to her too.

I offered to help carry her bags the rest of the way, and a few minutes later I was sitting in the living room of a big old house which backed onto the park, waiting to be brought a cup of tea. There were genuine-looking oriental carpets covering the floor and authentic-looking paintings covering the walls, but I couldn't have said if any of them were real. The room looked affluent and at the same time scruffy.

'Pssst,' I could hear behind me. 'Psssst!' Like someone trying to get attention in a cartoon.

I twisted around in my comfortable chair and saw an old woman clinging to the door jamb and beckoning. She was wearing a nightie and dressing gown. Her body looked so skeletal under the thin cloth, you wondered how she was still alive. She beckoned me to follow her and disappeared, then reappeared, beckoning more insistently. She was smiling, but her face was like a death's head, bright eyes deep in dark sockets.

There was no doubt it was me she meant. There was no one else in the room. I wanted to jump out the window. Instead I sat gaping and paralyzed. She padded across the carpet, touched my sleeve gently and indicated I should come with her. She had a medicinal smell. I got up like someone hypnotized and followed her down a long hallway to the back of the house. We walked past a bedroom with an unmade bed and clothes on the floor. I also saw a small sitting room – lots of books scattered around and a game show on TV. Still without speaking she led me to a narrow kitchen and pointed to a can of beans on the counter. An antiquated tin opener lay beside it. She did a lot of smiling and gesturing. I understood I was to open the tin. It wasn't easy. The opener was so old, it took a pair of strong hands. When I'd done she thanked me, nodding and bowing, and indicated that was all. Everything took place without a word. Then, just as I turned to leave, she said in a voice so weak I wasn't sure she'd spoken, 'I'm a prisoner here, you know.' This was followed by smiles and nods, as if being a prisoner here was the most sumptuous fate that could befall anyone. I fled back to the living room, where my hostess was waiting with a fat black teapot.

'I see you've met mother,' she said, sighing and shaking her head. 'I'm sorry if it was awkward.'

'No,' I said, thinking how scared I'd been. 'She's sweet. I helped her open a tin.'

'She is sweet – always was – but completely bonkers now.'

She apologised for not having biscuits. Several tears slid down her cheeks as she poured the tea. My chair suddenly didn't feel so comfortable. I wondered if this was a tea and sympathy trap. The tea itself was reassuring. It had a spicy aroma. Apple and camomile and something else. She poured it into big earthenware cups decorated with animals.

For a few moments we sipped our tea in silence, me waiting for the story of her shipwrecked life. To my relief it didn't come. We were soon interrupted by a croaking sound from the hall, followed by the appearance of a small, smartly dressed young woman speaking rapidly in what seemed to me Italian. My hostess started to introduce me in English, then realised she didn't know my name. So we exchanged names – Luke, that's me, and Nonn, that was her, and Maria, who turned out to be from South America. While we discussed the spelling and pronunciation of Nonn's Welsh name I stole curious looks at Maria. I have never seen a person who looked so much like a frog. I'm not being sexist or racist. The similarity was remarkable. She and Nonn conversed for a few moments in what I now took to be Spanish. Why, when you don't know the language, do people always seem to talk so fast? I caught something about a baby. Then Maria left the room.

'I brought Maria back with me from Peru,' said Nonn. 'Lately I couldn't have done without her. I was in hospital for a while with a post-natal psychosis. Really out of it, convinced I was going to die. Sometimes I thought I was my sister, who died when I was little.'

'I must have seen you in the Outpatients Clinic,' I said.

'Yes, I go for checkups, make sure my chemistry is OK. I'm not taking drugs, because I want to feed the baby. Maria fed her while I was in hospital. I thought I'd never get Ceri back on the breast. They're both amazing.'

On cue the amazing Maria entered carrying an enormous brown infant. Nonn shifted to a rocking chair and produced a large, pink, blue-veined breast, which the baby latched onto as if its life depended on it. 'This is Ceri,' she said. 'Her father is a carpenter, still in Peru.' I gazed at the snuffling Ceri. Then, hoping I hadn't been staring at her breast, I looked Nonn in the eye and she looked back. She had one brown eye and one blue.

'You have beautiful green eyes,' she said, rocking. And then, 'Why are you going to Outpatients?'

'I'm not anymore,' I said. 'I don't really want to talk about it.' But I thought maybe I did. I took a long sip of tea. The fragrance and the warm liquid were more than comforting. 'It's all right,' she said. 'I'm not usually so up front myself. I'm just in that mood today. I'm still amazed I asked you to help me cross the bridge.'

'Did it help? Crossing with me, I mean. Did it make a difference?'

'Oh, yes,' she answered. 'Not so much actually crossing. That still made me feel nauseous. But on the steps, knowing you were there, it prevented me having a panic attack. Hyperventilating. That sort of thing, which is really awful.'

'I had one of those exam breakdowns,' I said. 'Getting ready for finals. Mechanical engineering. I just cracked up. Couldn't sleep. Couldn't get my head straight. Then I started walking and couldn't stop. Nobody could live with me. I work... I'm a College guard now, what they call a transitional job. Eventually I'll go back to studying. Maybe English or law.'

'I had a walker in my ward,' she said. 'I remember she had terrible blisters.' She shifted the baby to her left breast and put the right one away. Her left breast looked tiny, like it couldn't possibly feed that gargantuan baby.

I gulped more tea. 'Why are your breasts such different sizes? Is it something to do with feeding the baby?' I couldn't believe I was having this conversation with somebody I'd just met, but it seemed perfectly natural.

'I used to play a lot of tennis,' she answered. 'I still do some coaching. My right side is overdeveloped.'

Sure enough, when I had a good look at her right forearm, it looked like Popeye, and the left, by comparison, like Olive Oyl. I glanced at her eyes again, blue and brown.

'The blue eye sees better than the brown,' she said, as if she knew my thoughts. 'It's some form of schizophrenia, isn't it? Walking?'

It was my turn to panic, again. 'It doesn't have a name. It has a number. Walking is the most obvious symptom. I walked for about eighteen months. They gave me really heavy drugs. My family thought I'd turned into Frankenstein's monster.'

'But you didn't see or hear things that weren't there?' she asked.

'I thought I was pregnant for a while, but I only told my sister.'

'She has children?' she said. She was good at the interrogative eyebrow.

'I don't think I was competing, if that's what you mean.' I felt the conversation was getting a little out of hand. There was a disturbance in the pit of my stomach which had nothing to do with digestion.

'So you had ECT?'

'Yes,' I said, remembering.

'And was it painful?' she asked. The more brutal her questions, the gentler her manner.

'No, just exhausting. The doctors think it worked. But they don't really know. I just realised one day I wanted out of there. Kind of decided it was better to be OK. I've got a release now, a piece of paper, and it more or less says I'm sane. I tease my friends, I'm the only one who can prove he's sane. I tell them they're all crazy, which they are. I don't mean they're ill.'

'No, I know.' Rocking, she shifted the baby back to the big breast, and it fell asleep. We sat in silence again. I thought how comfortable the silence was compared to when we were on the bus. I was feeling slightly churned up, but it was peaceful too, with Nonn rocking and nursing. Finally she said, 'More tea?'

'Thanks, I must get to work now.' I realised I was already an hour late. Such a crap job. But I liked some of the other guards, and I liked talking to the students. The building I'm in is designed so that the First Years are always lost and needing help.

Telepathically, Maria appeared and took the baby, and Nonn walked me to the door. The folds of her layered garments whispered. 'I hope I'll see you again,' she said. 'Here's my phone number.' She gave me a card that said something about tennis.

Just then, running silently along the hall from the back of the house, came the biggest dog I have ever seen. It was the size of a small pony. It looked like a St Bernard except it was black. It ran straight at me, leaped up, put its paws on my shoulders and started licking my face. Nonn, apologising profusely, got the dog down, scolded it and made it lie at my feet. The dog obeyed her quickly and quietly. Then it lay there with its heavy head on my foot and gazed up as if I were an object of worship.

'This is Lion. She's a Newfoundland,' she said, as if that explained everything. 'Mother must have let her in.' There were more apologies, and me saying no, no, I love dogs, and Nonn going on about how Lion was not only gentle and harmless but a certified therapy dog, approved to visit hospices and nursing homes. I got my foot out from under Lion's head, kneeled down and stroked her, just to show I did like dogs. Her coat was thick and cool. She rolled her eyes at me and turned over so I could scratch her tummy. She was a mammoth blotter that could soak up any amount of love. Eventually I stood up, and Nonn and I shook hands to say goodbye. She had a soft hand with a powerful grip. 'Why did you ask me to help?' I had to ask. 'I mean, you put the wind up me, sitting beside me like that, on an empty bus.'

She thought for a moment and smiled. She had a smile that seemed private rather than social.

'I don't know,' she said. 'I guess you made me feel safe. I can't explain it. You looked so patient.'

Then she put the palm of one hand on my chest, stood on tiptoe and with the other hand touched my cheek. She kissed me firmly on the lips. It went through me like ECT, only it felt good. I gazed into her weird eyes for what seemed a long time. Then I turned and went out the door and back to work.

PIRANHAS

They have nearly finished their seafood risotto, and she sips her wine and surveys the long, narrow restaurant hung with fishing nets and green glass floats. For such a dull-looking place it has unusually good food and drink. Their glasses of white wine shimmer, the colour of Umbrian sunlight on straw, just as it says on the bottle.

For the first time she notices the pair of fish in the tank next to them. They are beautiful but ugly as well. Their scales shine, iridescent, but their bottom jaws jut out and their top jaws are snubbed, making them look malevolent. And they have teeth.

She looks across at her dinner companion. Such a gorgeous man. How could she ever have thought he'd run off with her? He looks up, smiles and winks, glances around the restaurant and goes back to his food. His profile could be the head on a Roman coin. She wants to rub her fingers through his woolly white hair.

'A lot of men tonight,' he says. 'Maybe there was a match.'

'What are those fish?' she asks. 'They're lovely.'

'Piranhas,' he answers without looking up. 'In the back Gino has lots of them.'

'They couldn't be,' she says. 'The piranhas at the zoo look

99

as if they're made of mud. These sparkle like something off a Christmas tree.'

'A trick of the light,' he says, showing his perfect teeth. 'Gino knows about illusions.'

She looks at the fish again. That's exactly what makes me ugly, she thinks. The big underbite. She wonders whether it makes her look malicious too. If only her parents had been able to spend a small fortune on orthodontic surgery, she might have been beautiful. Well, pretty anyway. But she didn't need to be pretty. She was the clever daughter, who learned three languages. Perfectly.

He wrinkles his brow. 'I've got to be going soon. Bail conditions.'

'To be honest,' she says, lowering her voice, 'I didn't think you'd come tonight.'

'Why?' he exclaims softly, stuffing a forkful of pink risotto in his mouth and chewing, then pausing for effect. 'Why, in heaven's name? Tonight of all nights.'

'I was half-hoping you wouldn't come. That you'd already be gone.'

He becomes very still. 'I don't understand you.'

'Yes, you do,' she answers. 'And I understand you. And I don't blame you a bit.' Then she speaks to him in Spanish: 'I want to come with you.'

The man turns over some rice with his fork and stares at it. 'This evening Gino's risotto is a little sticky.'

Her underbite extends slightly further. 'The food is fine. Don't change the subject.'

'You talk in mysteries,' he protests. 'I love you. How could I not be here?'

'Because the police picked you up maybe?'

'That is nonsense. I am bailed by the police.'

Under the table his leg glides against hers. She gulps her wine, and her knees move apart. She knows he can see splashes of rose forming on the pale flesh of her neck. Can the fish see her blood moving? What they cannot see is how the pink spreads down her back and breast in a deep, hidden blush.

She takes a long breath and says, 'Just be careful. The British police are not as soft as you think. They'll pick you up for jaywalking if they can.' She leans forward and grips his knee under the table. 'The only one who thinks you're not going to jump bail is the judge.'

He looks her in the eye steadily, a long gaze, holding it until she glances away. She knows he does this when he wants to give an impression of complete sincerity. 'What is jaywalking?' he says.

She tries to think. If there is a Spanish word for jaywalking she can't remember it. 'What I'm saying is,' she continues, 'I don't want you coming back here. It's too big a risk. I want to join you. Out there. Wherever.'

'You will leave your husband?' His shapely dark eyebrows rise for emphasis.

'We left each other a long time ago. You know that. We only share a house now.'

'I will pay back the money,' he declares. 'I promise, on the soul of my mother.'

'The money is ours, yours and mine. Just let me know where you'll be.' She pauses. 'I know about your wife and children too. It doesn't matter.'

His face sets like a copper shield. She wonders if the conversation will turn nasty. The fish seem to be swimming faster now. They flash and glitter.

'I guessed that,' he says. 'I wanted no one to know. I wanted not to involve them. My wife and I are separate. Long time.'

'The police know. It was part of my briefing.' She thinks of the telephone tapes and wonders if he can tell when she's lying. She knows she's rattled him, because he is struggling with his English idiom.

'I must go,' he says again. 'Come to the restaurant. I leave a message with Gino.'

'When?'

'Soon.'

She takes another swig of wine and leans back and smiles. The underbite makes her smile look a little foolish. 'What does Gino know?'

'He is safe. He knows you are the love of my life.'

'Will he be hiding you in Italy?'

'Gino is not Italian. That is just an act, for the trade.' He takes another long drink, then holds his glass up to the light and studies it. 'This wine has integrity,' he announces.

'Tell me where you're going. Caracas? B.A.?'

'Best you not know. Then you do not lie to the police.'

'You think they know about us?' She has her shoe off and her foot in his crotch. The stiffness is satisfying.

'Be sure they will come asking questions.'

'I don't think so. I am trusted.' Her friends think it's glamorous, working as a police interpreter. They aren't the ones woken at all hours, typically three in the morning, travelling to another dreary clink, trying to construe the ramblings of some poor sod caught up in the law. In truth she prefers translating the manuals on industrial lubricants.

'They know you visit me in jail,' he says.

'On police business, yes. All proper and above board. The rest is safe.'

'Maybe I am followed. Maybe they know I speak English.'

'Oh, darling, delusions of grandeur. They haven't the manpower.' She grins, wriggles her toes and glances at her image in the wall mirror behind the fish tank. Her eyes twinkle, a deep, larkspur blue. She is proud of her eyes and knows how to use them. She puts her fair hand on top of his dark one, then removes it quickly. 'Us together. That is what I want.'

'And I too,' he says firmly, holding up his glass. 'To us.' He makes a toast, and they look into each other's eyes and drink. 'Go now,' she says. 'Don't wait for coffee. I'll get the bill.'

'Now I want to say goodbye properly.' He smiles like a scalpel, moving his hips.

'Say au revoir. I have a feeling you must go.'

'Why this feeling? Where is it coming from?'

'I can feel it in my water.'

'The police,' he says, 'they think I'm some kind of big drug czar.'

'You mean drugs baron.'

'What do you think? You know the drugs were planted.'

'I think they want you on some big charge. Trafficking or supply. I think you want to go away and stay away.'

The fish swirl the surface of the water. He gives her another long, probing look, then stands up quickly, blows her a kiss and goes out the door of the restaurant without looking back. The pain is instant, though she knows it will be worse when it has taken her over completely. She wants to jump up and rush out and escape with him, as if they were in some dark thriller. They would give police the slip in a fiendishly clever way, do a circuit of seedy hotels in unknown countries and in the end take a flying boat to some tropical spot where they would be happy and true to one another. She wants all this in spite of what she knows about his lies, his betrayal and true villainy.

She sees two young men in dark suits leave their table beside the toilet door and follow him out. Another man walks up to her table and stands over her. He is tall and barrel-chested and has bits of food around his mouth. She slips her foot back into her shoe.

'We got it, thanks,' he says quietly and gives her a cold grin that shows more food and a parade of bad teeth. 'A touch of entrapment, but well done.'

She gestures for him to come closer. He bends his large frame forward and she whispers, 'You snot-rag blackmailer, I don't want your thanks. Why have you blown my cover?'

'You sound like an old spy movie,' he hisses back. 'Don't worry about Gino. He bats for our side. You might thank me, saving you from a jail sentence.'

'So I can be murdered. Thanks hundreds and thousands.'

He straightens up. 'I'd better go. The boys will be nicking him now. Don't forget to return our equipment.' He goes out, and she beckons to Gino, the faux-Italian, who rushes over bowing and smiling. He has a serious tic in one eye. His smile looks like it is not connected with his brain.

'Bill, please, Gino.'

'No bill, Madame. On the house. Please have a coffee and a grappa.'

They exchange a look, and she decides she's earned it. 'All right. Thanks. Tell me, Gino, what sort of fish are those?'

'They are piranhas, Madame. The famous flesh-eaters.'

'From your home country?' she says in Portuguese.

Gino bows and gives another lobotomised smile, his tic tic-ticking. Then he turns on his heel and heads for the kitchen. The woman holds up her glass, and the last of the wine trembles, the colour of Umbrian sunlight on straw. She peers through the pale liquid at the two pugnacious-looking fish radiating light in the water. Their big lower jaws push through the weed. She moves her underbite back and forth, then side to side, and smiles.

VELMA

He was lost. Not lost as in trackless wilderness or endless ocean; he was lost as in leafy suburb, late for a dinner party. With the Baileys – Sophie and Bill. Did he even like them much?

He squinted and slowed the car to a crawl, searching for visual clues. Was that the Baileys' house, that big mock-Tudor across the road? There were so many half-timbered horrors in this place, behind all the overgrown trees and shrubbery. Slap a few boards on the front and you lived in Shakespeare's birthplace. A dark, four-legged thing scrabbled under a hedge – no doubt one of the large wild animals suburbanites called pets. He couldn't wait to get back to the city.

He pulled over, lowered his window and peered out at the dim, forested streets. No one about. A soft, autumn evening, beginning to grow misty over the lawns. He hoped there wouldn't be fog on the drive home.

No, that wasn't the Baileys'. Pulling forward, he stopped again at the entrance to a small cul-de-sac. Down at the end in a cosy ring of light stood an old-fashioned red phone box, the mock Georgian kind middle-class people fought savagely to preserve. He would have to try and phone.

His bag was still beside the front door of his flat, where he'd left it so he wouldn't forget when he went out. It held his mobile phone and address book, as well as the Belgian chocolates for Bill and the Cuban cigars for Sophie; he remembered they liked to reverse roles. Perhaps he should phone his ex – she'd know their number – but was she speaking to him?

He drove to the end of the cul-de-sac, got out and went into the phone box. He struggled to recall a number to dial. It was so long since he'd used a pay phone. Digging some coins out of his pocket, he gazed at the perfect sweep of lawn outside. What was the Baileys' address? Mottley Row. If he didn't know the street number, would they give him any information?

What he saw next seemed silly and unreal. He stood frozen, the phone receiver in one hand and a coin poised in the other. Across the expanse of lawn came leaping, galloping, a dark form that moved swiftly and noiselessly, heading straight towards him. Just as the thing seemed about to crash into his mock-Georgian refuge, it swerved to one side and executed a graceful leap through the open window into his car. The creature performed this strange, silent act in an effortless way, like something it did routinely every day.

It all happened quickly, but his imagination was quicker. He didn't see an ordinary black dog running past, but a gigantic, slavering hound. He imagined being trapped in this glass box for hours, the huge beast leaping out of his car, circling and baying until he could persuade the emergency services to come and help. No point in phoning the Baileys – they had a Chihuahua that bullied them.

He put the phone to his ear. Dead. Outside all was quiet.

No sound or movement. Stepping out of the box, he walked warily round the car, hanging back, bending over and peering inside. He could just make out the form of a large dog, light reflected on its black coat. It was sitting quietly on the back seat as if waiting for a ride. He winced when he thought of his taupe velour seat covers.

'Young man! What are you doing?'

He was so intent on the dog, he hadn't heard her come up behind him and almost jumped out of his linen suit.

'Are you one of those car thieves?' she said. 'Should I go into that phone booth and call the police?'

She was very small and very old. Her face was wrinkled and white, like it had been soaked for a long time in water. She was dressed in scarlet tracksuit bottoms and a scarlet top that said 'Wales' in big white letters. She wore luminous white trainers.

He started to stammer and ramble like a guilty man. He certainly was not a car thief. This was his car and how dare she? Then he noticed she was holding a dog lead. He quickly changed tack and asked, as politely as he could manage, if she was by any chance looking for her dog?

'Why?' said the old lady. 'Have you seen her?'

Pointing melodramatically, he announced, 'I think he's in the back seat of my car.'

'She's not a he!' she cried, rushing round the car, thrusting her head through the open window and shouting, 'Velma! What are you doing in there! Get out!' Then she turned on him again. 'Are you one of those pet thieves? Why have you got my dog in there?'

Before he could answer she threw open the car door,

108

snapped her lead on the dog's chain and, with a cry of 'Velma, you naughty girl!' followed by a torrent of genteel scolding, began a tug of war that Velma never looked like losing. The big dog hunkered down on the back seat and refused to budge, no doubt digging her claws into the taupe velour.

'What's the matter?' said the woman. 'Have you drugged her?'

'Madam,' he said in the stiffest manner he could muster, 'I am not a pet thief, car thief, or anything thief. I am an innocent bystander, with an unwanted dog in my car.'

'She is not unwanted! She is a much-loved dog!'

'I didn't mean it like that,' he said.

'Oh, I wish my husband was here. Help me!'

Wanting to do anything other than touch the dog, he suggested they help each other. He explained he was lost – did she know Mottley Row? – and her dog had jumped in his car while he'd been trying to phone. The tale sounded so unlikely he hardly believed it himself, but Velma's owner said simply, 'Yes, it's one of her favourite tricks.' He finished with a plea: if she could help him find the Baileys', he could give her and Velma a lift home.

'Yes, all right,' she answered. 'When we get home, Arthur can help.' And without hesitation, she climbed in his car.

Fifteen minutes that felt like fifteen hours later, they were parked on a main road outside a pub. Fields thick with ground fog stood opposite the pub – maybe a big school – but nothing looked familiar.

He was wondering whether to go into the pub and ask for directions. What stopped him, aside from the pub itself, which looked distinctly dodgy, was the police car pulled into a dark lane behind. No doubt waiting for drinkers to come out. Maybe the landlord hadn't contributed to the police retirement fund. Should he ask the cops where he was? How was he going to explain this strange old lady? By now he felt certain she was completely batty. She couldn't even find her own house. What if she told some bored constable that he was one of those kidnappers? What if she cried rape?

He peered across at his passenger. She looked like she'd gone into a trance. The orange streetlight reflecting on her pale face made her look eerie and alien. He checked the dog, lying placidly on the back seat. He'd spent the first few minutes driving around frightened she would spring and sink her fangs into the soft flesh of his neck, ripping out the veins and arteries. Or maybe just throw up on his seat covers. In fact the big pooch made no fuss at all and lay there like a lump, apparently happy to drive around all night.

'Where are we?' the old lady asked.

'That's what I'm trying to find out. Do you recognise this place?' She stared straight ahead.

'I want to go home.'

He ought to appeal to the police. What would he tell them? The truth? Couldn't he think of a more plausible version of events? He chickened out and started down the main road, aware he was driving at that funereal speed people use when there's a police car around. Despair struck when he looked in the mirror and saw the police pulling out behind him.

He turned off the main road hoping they wouldn't follow, but they did. What was the penalty for abducting a nutty old lady and her dog? Maybe he could persuade them he was a good Samaritan, which after all he was.

'Stop here!' she shouted. He pulled over, hoping he was off the hook. They were opposite a thickly wooded square. It might be a church square, but he couldn't see for the mist and trees. The police drove on past.

'Is this your house?' he asked. He gaped at the mock-Medieval pile facing them. It had vaulted battlements and even a round tower with crenellation. Maybe she'd escaped from the dungeon.

'No, I think I'm a bit lost,' she said. 'Drive to that corner and go right.'

After another five minutes of, 'Go right, now go left,' she turned around and said, 'Velma, where are we?' as if the dog could talk. Then she made a smothered noise. He pulled over and stopped the car. She was moaning as if crying, but there appeared to be no tears.

'I'm sorry,' she said. 'I've led you on a wild goose chase. I don't know what's the matter. I've lived here most of my life. It all seems strange.' With that she took his hand and held it against her cheek. Her cheek felt cold, but her hands were unexpectedly warm. 'You've been so kind,' she said. 'To me and Velma. You're so lovely.'

My God, was she going to kiss him? She was smiling up at him now, with higgledy-piggledy teeth, saying he was sweet. He extracted his hand. He couldn't dump her on the next corner, could he? What would he do with the dog?

Just then the police car pulled up behind him. A policeman got out and marched forward.

Almost relieved at the interruption, he decided to go on the offensive. Stepping out of the car he said, 'Excuse me, officer, we're a bit lost, my gran and I. Would you please direct us to

Mottley Row?' If only he could reach the Baileys, they might help him with the old lady. They might even know her.

'No problem, sir. Did you know you've got a defective tail light? It's showing white.'

He rushed round the car and displayed serious concern about his tail light. His breathing stopped, though, when he saw the old woman climbing out of the car and advancing toward the policeman. She halted in front of the big man in blue and looked up. Her white head was level with his brass belt buckle.

'Are you harassing this young man?' she said. 'He's trying to help me and my dog. We're lost.'

The policeman looked down and said, 'Just need to sort out this light, then you can be on your way.' He took out a pad of yellow forms and started writing.

'You're giving him a ticket? He's a good person.'

'It's only a warning, Ma'am. He'll take this to a garage and get his light repaired.'

The policeman glanced over and grinned at him when he pointed a finger to his head and made a few circles.

'I'm not crazy! I'm not!' she bellowed, and burst into tears, covering her face with her hands.

There was a terrible silence. To his surprise he felt genuinely ashamed. No one had ever called him a good person before. The old woman wept softly, and the big dog went frantic trying to get out of the car.

He was obliged to comfort his gran and apologise. He put his arm around her and steered her away from the policeman, giving her big hugs and fishing a handkerchief out of his pocket to dry her tears. 'Sorry, sorry,' he kept saying. He helped her back in the car, and she sat crying while Velma licked her wispy white hair.

Accepting his yellow form as if it were a winning lottery ticket, he had trouble listening to the policeman's directions. It wasn't a simple matter to follow them either, since Mottley Row turned out to be on the other side of town.

Ten minutes later they were cruising slowly along another leafy tunnel, and he was beginning to wonder if they were lost again, when Velma started to bark like a dog possessed. All he could think was what a deep voice she had – for a female, that is. Was he too going ga-ga?

Then the old woman started yelling, 'There it is! That's home!'

When he stopped the car she and the dog jumped out and ran across the grass into a large mock-Spanish house which looked like it was made out of bathroom tiles. That was that. Not so much as a by-your-leave. The porch light was on, and he saw them disappear through a fantastical wrought-iron gate. He sat there wondering if he ought to wait, make sure they'd got it right. He half expected an old man to come out and offer him a reward, or say he was charged with some disgusting crime.

He felt no surprise when he saw he was stopped across the road from the Baileys'. He gazed at the huge pile, remembering now its unique awfulness, a large Victorian house that combined Georgian, Tudor and Gothic features in one ghastly design. Its vacant, eye-like windows reminded him of something, probably a sinister nursing home in some horror film. He sighed, got wearily out of the car and walked up to the front door. Pinned on the heavy oak panel was a sign that read: 'Please do not ring bell, it hurts little Diego's ears. Strike knocker boldly.' He paused and wondered whether to turn around and go home. His finger hovered over the bell, sorely tempted. Then he steeled himself for an evening with Sophie and Bill, and little Diego. He took hold of the knocker and struck boldly.

MY DOG CAN TALK

Softly all of the urinals flushed, and the little blue cakes danced in the water. I was standing in the loo at the concert hall peeing and waiting for it to end. Not the concert, the peeing. The music had been lovely – cello and piano – and this was the interval. I stood listening to my trickle. One of the most tiresome things about being an octogenarian male is the length of time it takes you to pee, and the frequency you have to do it.

I was also humming to myself – the slow movement from the cello sonata I'd just been listening to – but behind me I could hear a murmuring. Someone talking. My upper body's still not too stiff to turn around while my lower half remains pointed at the bog, but when I did, no one was there. The door was shut to one of the stalls, and the monologue was coming from inside. Why should someone be talking to themselves in a public loo? At home I sat and muttered, but not where people could hear me. Wasn't that crossing the line, toward the sort who talk to themselves on the bus?

People who use mobile phones seem to talk anywhere, but I thought it unlikely you'd get a signal in the bowels of the concert hall, a cement box inside a concrete shell, with no windows. Or maybe there were two in there. Gay opportunists? A man with his child? I looked up at the surveillance camera and wondered who was observing me. I covered my dick with my hands. Was I really at risk from muggers and rapists? No one ever asked me if I wanted Big Brother watching. The peeing went on. And on. The murmuring went on too. But I couldn't make out the words. Of course I'm a bit deaf. Finally, with a glance at the camera, I squeezed out the last drips and quietly slipped into the cubicle next to the mumbler.

'I wish I had ears like yours,' he was saying. 'The high notes, low notes, undertones and overtones. I wish I could see what you see, but even more I wish I could hear what you hear. I wonder whether you hear the music I do, or something much more wonderful?' There was the sound of a fart, and then a splash as something hit the water. 'Most of it was conventional Romantic stuff, wasn't it? But the slow movement, that was exquisite, the cello strong and graceful like a Japanese bridge, with the piano flowing beneath.' He started humming the slow movement. He had a beautiful baritone voice, perfect for the cello part. There was a rattle and swish of paper as my stall was invaded by intestinal gas.

Then he stopped humming. I could hear a rustle of clothing and rapid, heavy breathing. His door opened, and he walked over to the sinks, accompanied by a strange clicking sound. I heard him use the tap, soap dispenser and blower. I just had to look.

I opened my door a crack and saw a small young man standing by the exit. In his left hand he held a long, slender, white cane, and in his right the leash to a small black-and-white dog which didn't look the least like a seeing-eye dog. It appeared to be a cross between a bulldog and some kind of terrier.

'My dog can talk, you know,' he said loudly and distinctly. 'But he doesn't like people eavesdropping. He won't say a word then.' He swung open the exit door and the air cylinder hissed. 'You should get a cat. Come on, Brian.'